# *KEEPING BOAZ*

## By Charles E. Davies

# CONTENTS

# ACKNOWLEDGMENTS

If it had not been the Lord who was on my side, where would I be? This excerpt from a song of degrees of David, found in Psalm 124, is indeed my testimony of God's Grace and Mercy. He is my All in All. I must admit before going any further that my life has been shaped thus far by a great number of people whose impact cannot be measured, nor described in words. First, to Gracie and Bolajeh Davies, I know you would have been proud of me. You taught me how to be empathetic while molding me in love and discipline as a gentleman. Thank you. Annie, Emeline, you have been there when no one seemed to care. And through it all, I'm glad to call you my sisters and friends. Thank you. To my uncles, Edmund and Joyomeg Vincent, I am still searching for the words to say how much I appreciate you. For now, if thanks are all I can give, then thank you. My journey in and passion for education started when you motivated me to be where you are. You may not know this: you inspired me and I adore you, Ruby Moigula. "You raised me up;" thank you for being the coolest cousin ever. The following people I can truly count on as friends; Araba Arthur-Mensah, Londa Lorton, Rachel Ansong, Rose Umoh, Magnus Georgestone, Dwight (Dax) Palmer, LaKeisha Strong, De'Cheryl Swift, Nicole Glover, Laura Thiesen, Susan Sura, Franklin and Violet Coomber; you are. Thank you for being friends indeed. To Rev. Clifford L. Herd and his wife Nancy, thank you for opening your heart and welcoming me into your world. Your words of encouragement, biblical counseling, and warmth mean more to me than I can express. To my adopted parents, Mr. & Mrs. Cecil Strong and Mr. & Mrs. John Umoh, whose sacrifices and kindness cannot be measured in smiles, hugs or labor of love, I'd like to say, thank you. You have a good heart and may God continue to bless you and your family in all your endeavors.

To those who afforded me the opportunity during our counseling sessions of guiding them in matters of the heart, thank you. To all the ministers and lay leaders who've taught me over the years to trust in God, stay in his word, and through whose anointed teachings I exercise my faith and wisdom, I must acknowledge you. For though sometimes it would have seemed that your words were going unheeded, the Holy Spirit in his wisdom was preparing the fallow ground of our hearts. Be encouraged, for I attest this day that your labor was not in vain; as out of many, I am one. Last but certainly not least, to my pastor, father in the faith and friend, Bishop David G. Evans, I'd like to say, thank you. I have traveled this world and visited with and sat under a good number of Christian leaders, and still I have no qualms in saying that you are the greatest teacher I know. As a spiritual father, through your obedience to the word and will of God, unknowingly, you took over where my parents left off and have since guided me in my walk with the Lord, molded my thinking as a man of God, and challenged me to live a holy life worthy of God's calling. You are in my every prayer, and I thank God for you and your ministry.

It is with deep humility that I pause to acknowledge those who've sacrificed of their love and time to make this publication a success. To my editor, Michelle Levigne; graphic designers; author service representative; and Tracy K. Sullivan, my publishing consultant, I gracefully yield that if not for your professionalism and quality of work, this novel would still be among the few waiting on the sidelines of my flash drives to be accessed. Thank you so much for the updates, follow-ups and relentless attitude in seeing this project through, and your tireless work in making sure this book of wisdom takes flight.

# PROLOGUE

Ruth Moore, an RN, and shift supervisor at the Green Meadows Nursing Home (GMNH), had given up on love and settled down to raising her two sons, Brian and Marcus, as a single mother. Her romantic life had been a comedy of errors. She had seen and done it all: from "going steady" during her high school days to becoming a "main squeeze"; from hopping in and out of "exclusive relationships" to being involved in some so-called "serious relationships"; from crying through her uncommitted "committed relationship," to a place in time where all she could show for it were two boys with different dads and an abrupt marriage.

Ruth's path in life crossed with that of Naomi Parsons, a widow in her mid-to-late seventies and resident at GMNH, who at first could offer nothing but words of wisdom to Ruth. Reluctant to get attached to residents at the nursing home, through her sympathy for Naomi, Ruth developed a friendship that transformed her life and taught her that there was more to a lasting relationship and marriage than love. As Naomi inquired: "So, let me get this straight, you can attract your Boaz but you just can't keep him?" This question is true of many singles who have no problem attracting others into their sphere through: beauty, accomplishments, social standings, prosperity and even religiosity. However, maintaining their relationships is where the staples come unhinged as varying decisions are made and guided by a mindset not based on the Word of God. Encouraged and challenged by Naomi to love again, Ruth accepted an invitation for a date with Dr. Otis Swift and the two found a common chord in love. In applying Naomi's wisdom, Ruth developed from a woman to a lady, and from possessing worldly tendencies to a life of faith.

This novel presents an allegorical account of the life of the biblical character, Ruth, as she progresses through her internal struggles and complex relationship with Naomi, who guides her in wisdom and grace while navigating the currents of love in her romance with Dr. Swift. For those unfamiliar with the Old Testament's biblical narrative (in four chapters) of the Book of Ruth (though not required), a brief reading would help capture the prevailing themes in Ruth's life.

The cover design (interlocking wedding bands in a triangle) is symbolic of our ultimate goal which is that of having a blessed union or marriage that is anchored in the triune God or Holy Trinity. It reflects a union between a husband, his wife and God. This triple bottom line is a threefold cord weaved in God's anointing. It is embedded in the belief that the vows made by the husband and wife to each other are in reality made by the husband to God and his wife; and the wife to God and her husband. The interlocking wedding bands in the triangle also serves as a reminder that we are not inviting God into the marriage but that he is an integral part of the marriage...everything in this union is and should be channeled through God.

This novel can be used as a guide in conducting successful relationships and guarding against internal and external forces that tend to gradually erode established unions. It seeks to reaffirm some common sense and conventional wisdom approaches we sometimes take for granted in building and maintaining a trustworthy relationship. It is my prayer that this literature would both minister to and confirm in the spirit of all readers biblical truths and applied knowledge where most needed in our walk with God and relationship with each other.

# FOREWORD

C harles Davies is a committed Christian who uses his God-
given gifts in writing to recast the biblical story of Ruth and
Boaz into a modern-day novel. This novel brings you into the life
of a modern-day Ruth with her hurts and failed relationships. Ruth
meets Naomi, and in the growing relationship allows herself to be
open to Naomi's guidance and wisdom.

This novel keeps you involved in the unfolding story as you
see Ruth's growth in a new relationship. Through Naomi's love
and direction, Ruth prepares for a deeper, more lasting, Christ-
centered relationship with her new husband. Charles Davies shares
much insightful wisdom in this novel for both men and women.
He includes a "Wisdom Journal" that was kept by Ruth, as Naomi
shared with her some invaluable words of wisdom during their
growing relationship.

I would recommend this book as required reading for those in
pre-marital courses, as well as those considering marriage. It is a
fascinating novel that also offers helpful insights for those already

married. It is enjoyable reading and has a strong biblical base with guidance and direction for establishing and maintaining solid marital relationships. "If your marriage is God-ordained, then make it God-maintained."

Thank you, Charles, for sharing your gifts in this intriguing novel!

Rev. Clifford L. Herd, MDIV. MEd.
Retired Lutheran Pastor and Counselor

# ABOUT THE AUTHOR

C harles E. Davies is a sinner saved by grace; enlightened in sharing the wisdom gleaned from his years of counseling experience, ministries, and life's experiences with you as a reader.

# DEDICATION

To those who believed and prayed in faith; especially

my friend unlike any other,

Dr. André L. Hines.

# PART I

# LOVE'S RESOLVE

# The Crossroad

*"Accept the things to which fate binds you, and love the people with
whom fate brings you together, but do so with all your heart."*
— *Marcus Aurelius*

"Nurse Moore, you have a call on line two," the front desk clerk softly noted as she leaned into the room where Ruth was standing over her patient.

"Thank you…is it an emergency?" Ruth asked.

"It sounds like it's from one of your boys."

"Tell him I will call them shortly…thanks," Ruth said, as she smiled in appreciation at the clerk.

Ruth, a single mom, always left whatever she was engaged in to attend to calls from her two sons, Brian, fourteen, and Marcus, eleven. The boys usually called after school to let her know they'd made it home safely, and this day was no different. They were the joy of her life. She would have picked up the call and asked them about their day, and if they had started working on their homework assignments from school, but this time it was different. Her patient,

Mrs. Parsons was not in any critical condition, but she was offering something; something Ruth considered priceless. She was offering Ruth wisdom.

Ruth, a registered nurse and shift supervisor at the Green Meadows Nursing Home (GMNH), had come to develop a strange relationship with Mrs. Parsons, a beautiful and graceful lady in her mid-to-late seventies who had developed osteoporosis over the years. Her husband for fifty-seven years, Elliot, had passed away from Alzheimer's a couple of months ago, and their two sons, Larry and Edwin (who also happened to be members of the nursing home's board of trustees), thought it was best that mom be moved over to the nursing facility, where she would have company, and be taken care of; especially after her last fall, in which she fractured her hip. Mrs. Parsons had moved into GMNH the previous week and always wanted to strike a conversation with anyone who walked into her room. She always wanted to tell them about her love, Elliot. She missed him.

Ruth had learned not to get attached to the patients and tried to distance herself from their personal lives; particularly after the passing of one of the nursing home's residents, Mr. Walton, whom she had come to respect as a fatherly figure over the years. Word had gotten to Ruth, when she reported for work on the second shift (3 – 11pm) that the new resident was a talker, so she tried very hard not to linger around Mrs. Parsons' room that day any more than required. The following day, however, Mrs. Parsons had requested to speak to the supervisor since the soup served was a little too salty for her to take in, even though she had kindly informed the dietician of her preference. Taking a deep breath, Ruth left her station and walked reluctantly over to Mrs. Parsons' room to render her assistance. Upon entry, Mrs. Parsons took off her reading glasses, put down her Bible, and squinted at Ruth's nameplate.

"Nurse Moore," she quietly started. "By the way, if you don't mind me asking, is that your maiden name? Because it was mine, before Elliot and I got married."

"No, Mrs. Parsons. It was from a previous marriage," Ruth courteously replied, with a smile.

"Oh, I am sorry to hear that," continued Mrs. Parsons. Extending her hand to greet Ruth, she added, "Just call me, Naomi."

Reciprocating by shaking Naomi's hand, with a warm smile, she replied, "Ruth."

"Oh goody!" exclaimed Naomi. "If I had a son who was single, it would have been perfect," she joked. "Anyway, are you the supervisor? I had called to see if you can help the dietician get it right… the sodium, my dear, the sodium…it's just too much for me to take in," she moaned.

"I will make sure they get it right the next time," Ruth replied with an apologetic smile. "Is there anything else I can do for you while I am on a roll?"

"Well, since you've asked," she replied, smiling, "can you stop by when you are less busy for just a few minutes? I'd like to show you something."

"I sure will, and it was nice meeting you, Naomi," Ruth stated, as she left the room.

Taking a walk down to the kitchen, Ruth thought, *Wow, she is a really nice lady.* Entering the kitchen, she requested that Naomi's dietary needs be given special attention, since she was a patron of the home. The day was fairly uneventful, and it was about 8pm when Ruth decided to check on Naomi to see if the sodium level in her dinner was acceptable, and also to take a look at what Naomi wanted to show her. Excited at the visit, Naomi said her dinner was delicious, and proceeded to reach into her handbag and take out her photo album. She pointed Ruth to a chair, asked her to come closer, and the two went through the sixteen still photos Naomi's weary album could hold. Each photo was a story of joy and life; a journey of beauty and hope; and a triumph of love, the memories held dear to her heart of her lost love, Elliot. Naomi was very appreciative of the time Ruth had spent with her, and in tears told her she was lonely without Elliot. After his passing, she didn't have a friend in the world and pretty much had given up on finding one.

Touched by the sadness in Naomi's eyes, as her thin lips quivered from the pain of loneliness, Ruth reached out for a tissue by the bedside, wiped Naomi's face, and said, "Don't cry...I will be your friend." Staying a little longer than anticipated, Ruth took the time to brush Naomi's hair, pulled it back, freshened her for the night, kissed her on the cheeks and wished her good night.

Ruth was moved by the love Naomi and Elliot shared, the love she had always dreamed of, but like trapping lightening in a bottle, love had evaded her throughout all her adult life. In seven months, she would be turning that dreaded "Four - O"...yes, forty years old and still without a man in her life. Ironic and as if by divine humor to the day in September that she was born, Ruth had worked all her adult life ...and this Labor Day birthday was shaping up to be a hard one for her to bear. *Well, at least I have Brian and Marcus,* Ruth thought, as she left the nursing home that night. With her sons, Ruth was never alone, but in the hollow confines of her mind, the whispers of her loneliness called out for a companion. As she drove home that night, she was torn between two worlds...one of hope in knowing that love could exist between two people, such as that shared by Elliot and Naomi, and then there was her world...a world where love was but a fleeting image.

For Naomi, it was a good night...the first good night in a long time. She slept well and expectantly woke up early the next morning, pestering the nursing home's staff about when Nurse Moore would be back at work. Naomi had found a friend...not one to replace Elliot, but someone she could talk to...someone who would listen. She was told that Nurse Moore worked the second shift, and sometimes both second and third shifts, but didn't work on weekends, or the first shift.

# Reflections

*"Adversity does not make us frail; it only shows us how frail we are."*
— *Abraham Lincoln*

After the boys left for school the next day, later that morning, propped up in bed with her coffee in one hand and watching *Wheel of Fortune*, Ruth's mind wandered in agony through the dark alleys of her failed relationships. She thought of Naomi's blessed life of love that she shared with Elliot, and wanting to reciprocate by sharing her life with her new friend. Stumbling off the bed, Ruth reached across to the TV stand and removed some old magazines from the bottom shelf that were sheltering her past, her photo album. Dusting it off, she decided to take out some pictures of her and the boys, which she could share with Naomi. As she turned the leaves of her life, she could hear the cries of promises lost, see the sadness of romances failed, feel the pain of hopes aborted, and smell the guilt of bar scenes with ghosts of pledges of a lifetime that died with the neon lights. She saw herself in the arms of strangers who promised love, but left her wishing for death. She hurriedly turned the pages from her time with Magnus, only to open up the memories of her ordeal with Jason.

*If only time could heal all wounds*, Ruth thought. She once found it hard to believe that love could hurt, and that being in an abusive relationship only happened to others, for she was a strong woman and no man would ever make her wish for death. Ruth once had a thing for the proverbial "bad boy"; you know, the one who couldn't care less and was accountable to no one. As if caught in a trance and looking from the outside in, Ruth stared at pictures of herself, all nestled in the arms of a love she never had. Jason had moved in with Ruth shortly after spending the night and had refused to leave. Even though she was the only wage earner (at least legally) in their love pad, Ruth at first found it endearing that she had a man who made her love come tumbling down, for they were physically compatible. But as the weeks progressed, Jason grew possessive and frequently lashed out at Ruth for the slightest of reasons. It first started with obscenities, then a collar choke, and later manifested in slaps and kicks. Jason always apologized after those episodes, and was so skilled in it that even Ruth started thinking of herself as the instigator and victimizer.

Better judgment wanted him to leave, but Ruth had convinced herself that it was better to have someone by her side than to be alone as other single women; considering the "shortage of good men," which in her case was skewed at best. The people in her circle tried to warn her and advise her as to leaving, but she always turned them off with her same excuse: "But he loves me." Gradually, Ruth was demoralized to the lowest point in her life, where a stare could keep her from even going outside to check the mail. She feared the worst but could not tell a soul, for shame and guilt were home. Nine months, three weeks and four days later, after much despair, Ruth got the cops to escort him out of her home; but not before leaving the skin of her upper left arm in his nails, while tugging away from his grip.

Jason never returned, but left a psychological scar that still sometimes woke Ruth up in the middle of the night in a panic, all drenched in sweat.

She skipped a few leaves on the album…but then there was Donald…as if the pain would never end…she flipped over and entered her life with Hamed, Brian's dad. This was the time she decided to try a different race, only to conclude that "men are all the same" as far as she was concerned. Hamed had fallen off the face of the Earth after Ruth caught him in bed with one of her girlfriends. Shaking her head in remorse, with saddened eyes, Ruth's thoughts engulfed her.

She had gone through the "It's not you, it's me"; the "I need my space"; the "Don't call me, I'll call you"; the "I don't see any future in our relationship"; and even the one she later realized shared the same affinity with her, for the male sex. Shaking her head in regret, Ruth once more tried to do something that lately had left her feeling disgusted with herself, a task she found hard to complete: accounting for all the failed relationships in her life, not including the tryst that left her asking the question, "What am I doing?" This time was no different. She broke down in tears after reaching double digits. It was a painful tribute to her poor choices, and there was still a quarter more of this self-indicting prosecution in still frames to go.

This final quarter was one of self-improvement. After Brian was born, Ruth had decided to make something better of herself, so she went to nursing school while balancing her life as a single mother, and working full-time to provide for her son. Beaming smiles appeared in pictures of her graduation from a Licensed Practical Nursing Program (LPN). But oh no, there was Duncan, "Mr. Abusive" himself. Like Jason, he had promised Ruth the moon and stars, but got abusive and extremely violent when he didn't have his way, as their relationship regressed. He ended up stealing from Ruth and pawned her jewelry to support his drinking and drug habits before disappearing. He was Marcus's dad.

Between the last page of her tribute to disappointments and the hardened cover of her painful past was a solitary funeral memorial service program with the smiling face of Marlon. He was a good one. He really loved Ruth, but had passed away from some internal complication, six months after they got married. But for this funeral program, Ruth had tried to destroy and erase anything that would remind her of their time together as this was a painful time for her; the period in which she erected her wall of solitude, in which she resolved to abandon love and its shadows, and just take care of her sons.

Lost in this panorama of despair were the pictures of Ruth and Bradley. After their bitter separation, Ruth had torn all the pictures she had of him, and burned everything she could lay her hands on that reminded her of that time in her history when the thought of love hurt her; even songs on the radio clouded her day as the memories lingered. After a night of passion, Ruth, as a "liberated woman" had even proposed to Bradley, thinking that he would finally learn to love her if she gave him all she had and loved him with more passion. No matter how hard she tried, he treated her badly until she had forced him to attend a counseling session. There, it was revealed to Ruth that people usually put their best foot forward when dating, and if this was the best that Bradley could do, marrying him would be a grave mistake. She refused to believe that her investment in love had negative returns, but Ruth later realized that unfortunately while she was looking for a lover, Bradley wanted nothing more than a casual relationship or friendship. The thought of that nudged her into anger.

To meet all her bills and responsibilities, Ruth had gone back to school based on advice from Mr. Walton, the patient who had meant so much to her. The last picture trapped in this cage of humiliation was from her graduation as a registered nurse. Other than two passport-sized pictures of the boys, which she carried in her purse, a couple of full-sized pictures from their school's photo shoot, and a portrait of her and the boys, taken one Sunday after church, there wasn't much to show. Able to pull out nine pictures of her and her sons, Ruth sighed, just thinking about the opposite ends of the spectrum in which she and Naomi found themselves. Her pictures weren't as admirable as Naomi's, but this was all the love she knew. The love from Brian and Marcus was all she had.

Other than the parental love she had from her dad after her mom left them, when growing up as a girl in Brooklyn, NY, her romantic life had been a comedy of errors. She had seen and done it all: from "going steady" during her high school days to becoming a "main squeeze"; from hopping in and out of "exclusive relationships" to being involved in some so-called "serious relationships"; from crying through her uncommitted, "committed relationship," to a place in time when all she could show for it were two boys with different dads and an abrupt marriage. Deep down inside, even though Ruth was resigned to being single, she knew she would be happier in a relationship for a myriad of reasons; the least of which wasn't love.

Around midday, Ruth prepared dinner for her sons and decided to leave early for work so that she could spend some time with Naomi. As she stood by the bed while getting dressed, she reflected on her life and wondered out loud, "Where did I go wrong?" As if beckoned by the mirror, Ruth slightly turned her head, and for the first time in a long time, her figure captured her attention. Ruth knew she was beautiful. She could have been a model, at 5' 9", blemish-free skin, golden-brown complexion, dimples that would make even Caligula blush, long shiny black hair with no split ends, penetrating eyes with naturally neat lashes, her breasts, stomach, and thighs still firm.

"I look good enough to be a model...so, what is wrong with me?"

Growing up, Ruth wanted to be a wife, mother, and career woman so badly, just like the ladies she read about in the magazines, and saw on TV...but now she had to settle for two out of three.

"Is it too much to ask?" she quietly questioned. "I pray, attend services when I can, occasionally volunteer in ministry, keep myself holy as best as I can, so why? What am I missing? There are nice and decent men in church...but it seems like every other month, someone else is getting married, but me. It has now come to the point where I am even avoiding social functions that require couples to attend. Did I miss my husband while I was out in the world? Is God paying me back for the life I've lived?"

She couldn't help but sob as she stared into the mirror at the reflection of the Ruth her "friends" and ex-lovers preferred...the one who was weak and a failure. She watched her mascara run down her cheeks, again. Pulling herself together as she had done these past eleven years, Ruth got dressed, reapplied her makeup, and with tear-filled eyes took some time out to write a love note to her sons before leaving for work.

Arriving at work a little earlier than usual, Ruth was greeted by a barrage of silly comments from her co-workers, joking over Naomi's concern for her new friend. Smiling, she jokingly told them to stop being jealous, and to find a friend of their own. Walking over to Naomi's room, Ruth was also excited about her new friend. She had made a commitment that she intended to keep: to be a friend to this precious lady. Exhausted from the anxiety of a day of longing to see Ruth, Naomi had dozed off, but was surprisingly awakened by Ruth's voice in the corridor. Upon entering Naomi's room, Ruth apologized for not informing Naomi of her scheduled hours and promised to do better. She then pulled up a chair next to Naomi and asked about her day. As if the floodgates opened, Naomi spent the next forty-five minutes telling her about everyone who attended to her that day, her breakfast, lunch, and even some of the comments she overheard about the other patients in the home.

When she had to punch in for the start of her shift, Ruth gave Naomi the pictures that she had brought in from home, and promised to stop by when on her break. Happy and eager to know more about Ruth, Naomi took the pictures and settled in to carefully and lovingly admire Ruth's family. Later that evening, Naomi's two sons visited their mother. She called Ruth in and introduced her as their new sister. She told them that Ruth was the supervising nurse in the second shift and that she had been taking very good care of her. The men were grateful for their mom's new outlook and thanked Ruth and her staff for the wonderful work they were doing.

During her break later that evening, Ruth visited Naomi, and the two ladies sat down and went through Ruth's photos, as promised. With every picture, Naomi noticed the chords of joy and sadness that strummed through Ruth's emotions as she spoke admirably of how smart and disciplined her sons were, while silently screaming of the disappointments in her life. She felt the tears of pain that flowed down Ruth's cheeks as she smiled and boasted of how both boys had made the President's list in school the past two semesters, and were also members of the varsity football team. Ruth took the last picture and stared at it for a while before handing it to Naomi as she narrated the backdrop. She stared as if looking for an image; an image that wasn't there. It was a picture the three of them had taken after church on a Sunday afternoon. The boys were a lot younger then, but the picture still revealed the truth about Ruth's life. It was a portrait of a beautiful and attractive lady with her two sons, one on each side...but there was a space that no one filled, a space for the husband she prayed she had.

Shortly after finishing her story about the portrait, Ruth's break time expired. She gathered the pictures, which were now spread over Naomi's blanket, and asking for forgiveness, Ruth kissed Naomi goodbye and went back to work. Saddened by her new friend's despairing hope for love, Naomi walked down the memory lane of her fifty-seven-plus years of a rich and fulfilling love life with Elliot, and appreciatively thanked God for his blessings towards her.

After clocking out that night, Ruth stopped by Naomi's room to say goodnight, but she was fast asleep. Ruth drove home that night with a heavy heart. She couldn't put her finger on it...but there was a hole, a pit of grief, in her heart. She suppressed the emotions of past disappointments as she usually did, because the boys sometimes waited up for her; and she hated herself whenever they saw her crying, especially after Marlon's death. Her sons meant the world to her.

The week flowed by uneventfully, with Ruth and Naomi getting to know each other as their conversations were filled with the love, laughter, and joy Naomi and Elliot had shared. Saturday would mean not seeing Naomi until Monday afternoon. *Oh no,* Ruth thought...*I didn't even say goodbye or wish her a great weekend.*

Saddened at the thought of Naomi's disappointment, she got the boys dressed up early that afternoon and told them she was going to introduce them to their Mom's new best friend. Anything to get out of the house on a sunny day, the boys agreed, knowing they could also milk a dinner and a movie out of this deal. They arrived at GMNH to surprised looks from the staffs over how Brian and Marcus had grown since the last time they visited. People also wondered what brought Ruth to the home on a weekend. She explained that she was just visiting a good friend, and walked up to Naomi's room.

Naomi's eyes lit up when she saw Ruth and the boys. They were very handsome young men, she thought, and gave Ruth a motherly smile of approval at the way she was raising her sons.

They visited for three hours, during which the boys got to hear stories about Elliot and Naomi's two sons, while telling Naomi about their school, favorite subjects, and ambitions in life. Ruth and the boys left Naomi with a promise to give her a call on Sunday. They spent the rest of the day having a late lunch and watching two movies at the theatre, before returning home and settling down to get some rest in time for church on Sunday. It was a good and very pleasant day for Ruth and the boys.

Consistently inconsistent in her walk with God, until Naomi, Ruth had a hard time believing God could be a "friend that sticketh closer than a brother" after all the bitter pills in life she had to endure. It somehow became more of a ritual, an occasional appearance to appease her conscience, or as church lingo had taught her, "the Holy Spirit," and this Sunday was no different. It was church time again, a day Ruth sometimes dreaded, at the thought of attending service without a husband by her side. She watched the married women clinging to their husbands as if threatened whenever the single ladies walked by. It had been a very trying relational path for Ruth in the church. She had the bitter epiphany after the second relationship with a "Christian Brother" that ministry didn't make the man. Neither Minister Aaron nor Deacon Mitchell was willing to stand for God when presented with the choice between living a holy and a carnal lifestyle. Even the Singles Ministry was a challenge for Ruth, as she discovered after a month of active participation that less than two percent of the single men in the church attended. The age range of females in the Singles group got younger with each enrollment, and graduating out of the class by means of finding a life partner was as likely for her as the sun rising in the west. The church had a good number of single women, but looking around, it was obvious that age had kept its course while these ladies were fasting and praying for their soul mate, that "holy" and "anointed" brother whom God would send their way.

*Take Evangelist Carol for example: once secretary for the Singles Ministry and now somewhere in her mid-to-late sixties. It's like they grew weary of fasting and praying for a love they couldn't find, and so they resigned themselves to living for God. I am sure that's not what God had in mind, I am sure he doesn't want to be a "second best,"* Ruth thought.

After service that day, Ruth called to impress Naomi with her church attendance and to chat for a few moments. Naomi, however, had visitors; her sons and their families were visiting, so she promised to return Ruth's call later that evening. Naomi had four grandchildren; two boys from Larry, and a set of twin girls from Edwin. They were lovely children, and so were their mothers; Tammy, Larry's wife of six years, and Stacy, Edwin's wife of four years. Naomi loved her family and was proud of her sons.

Ruth spent the afternoon with her boys, going over their school's weekend assignments while doing the laundry. She watched them iron their clothes for the coming week as she prepared lunch and dinner for the two. Knowing her girlfriend would be calling later, she hung out with her sons and watched a movie, expectantly waiting for Naomi's call.

# The Question

*"Continuous effort - not strength or intelligence - is the key to unlocking our potential." - Winston Churchill*

Later that evening, around seven-thirty, after Naomi had her fill of her family, she settled down to call her new best friend, Ruth. Long-winded as Naomi was, Ruth could also hold her own. The two ladies talked for hours about life, family, their Christian walk, but mostly about Elliot. Around 10pm, when Naomi had worn herself out with the day's excitement and her conversation with Ruth, and before saying goodnight, she asked Ruth a question that was long overdue. It was a question Ruth had heard before…a question her dad used to ask her every fortnight before passing away a couple of years ago.

"Ruth!" Naomi began. "You are a very attractive and beautiful young lady. You are kind and courteous, any mother would want you for her son, and I've seen the way Dr. Swift looks at you when he comes around. Even my sons had to do a double take when they first saw you. Ruth, Baby…I consider you my daughter. Honey, you've got two handsome and very intelligent sons…why don't you do those boys a favor and find them a dad? They need a male figure in their lives."

There was a deafening silence.

"Ruth, are you there?" Naomi asked.

Slowly finding the response to a question whose answer had always evaded her, Ruth tearfully replied: "I don't know. I don't know what's wrong with me. I have tried…I really have…I have let my sons down so many times, I decided to stop hurting them. They are too young to go through the pain of a breakup. You know, they get so easily attached…and it hurts me to see them heartbroken when these men walk away."

Naomi was sad for her friend, and wished she was near to hug and comfort her. She couldn't even find the words to ease the pain. Naomi wished she knew the words to say to someone who had tried and failed. It was hard for her, lying in that bed and feeling helpless. Swallowing the lump in her throat, Naomi asked Ruth to come in an hour early on Monday, so that they could have some time to talk before her shift started.

After they hung up, Ruth dried her tears, washed her face, brushed her hair, and put on some makeup to mask her sad countenance. She walked over to the boys' room, told Marcus to scoot over, sat by his side of the bed, grabbed his children's Bible and proceeded to read Matthew's account of the "Sermon on the Mount" to the boys, until they fell asleep. Ruth always tried to read a passage of scripture to the boys before going to bed. She found this to be comforting for them, even though she was ashamed to admit she didn't really believe in the God she was trying to teach her sons about. But she thought it best to have her sons be channeled into manhood through the church instead of a street gang or even the "Y." Ruth loved and cared for her sons greatly. With no father figure in their lives, she sometimes took the boys down to the church so that they could hang out with some of the deacons and ministers.

The boys only had a few friends Ruth could tolerate, and so they had learned over the years not to invite other people into their home when Ruth was not around, and to always make sure their decisions or activities in school did not earn them a request for their mom to come down to the school, or get them sent to the principal's office for disciplinary actions.

With a heavy heart, Ruth then went down to the kitchen, and prepared the boys' lunch and dinner for the next day. After making sure that her home was secured, she turned the lights off and went upstairs to bed. That night was very difficult for Ruth. All she thought about was her past relationships. She gave all she knew how, but somehow love, like oil, floated above the water of her life.

The alarm clock went off at 5:30am. Ruth had swollen eyes from tears and a sleepless night as she woke the boys up for school, reminded them to do their push-ups (an exercise Ruth and her sons had come to respect as part of their daily routine, because it kept them alert throughout the day), went downstairs to the kitchen and prepared breakfast for her sons. After breakfast, the boys helped with the cleaning, took out the trash, got dressed, said their prayers, kissed Ruth goodbye, and left for school.

Watching her sons as they walked off to catch the bus, a heavy sadness came over her. She felt alone and lonely. It was like Brian's first day of preschool, as she watched the school bus pull away with her baby in it; and was left alone, pregnant in an apartment full of toys. The solitude that breathed emptiness engulfed Ruth. It felt as if her love was screaming, "Let me out!" from behind the walls of the dark chamber of her heart, filled with the wreckage of her pasts. She felt like someone stumbling to a cracked window, only to see that broken hearts like tumbleweeds and faded tracks of fleeting romances were all that was left in her world to love. Crying uncontrollably, Ruth locked the kitchen door, turned the alarm on, and went back upstairs to her bedroom, where she cried herself to sleep.

# The Conversation

*"It is never too late to be what you might have been."* —*George Eliot*

Waking up at 12:30 that afternoon with a piercing headache, Ruth dragged herself out of bed and walked into the bathroom. There she saw the familiar Ruth...the one with no makeup, puffy eyes, swollen face, and hair unkempt. Bracing herself, she took a cold shower, after which she put on her makeup, got dressed, and headed off to work. Ruth got there at 1:45pm, and walked up to Naomi's room. The woman was relieved to see her friend once again.

"Oh, Darling," Naomi began, "am I glad to see you. I was worried about you...are you okay?"

Smiling, Ruth replied: "I am so sorry...I don't know what came over me...I didn't mean to upset you."

"No, no, no," exclaimed Naomi. "You didn't upset me...come let me give you a hug...hmm! And you smell great, too." Smiling, she continued, "Whatever you are going through, you wear it well...

pull up a chair." Smiling at Ruth, and beaming with delight, she continued: "I missed you, this past weekend...am I glad to see you... you make a difference in this nursing home...you sure do...the place was just not the same...anyway, enough about work...tell me, dear, are you really okay?"

"Yes," replied Ruth. "I am fine now." And holding Naomi's hand, she looked into her eyes...the eyes of love and comfort... those olive eyes of experience and reassurance. Feeling appreciated and cared for, Ruth surrendered. "Thank you for being my friend."

"No...thank you!" replied Naomi, who then continued, "I understand...breaking up is hard on children...but what do you want?"

Ruth gave a sigh while looking down at the checkerboard floor in disappointment, and slowly shaking her head in regret. Sensing her friend's hopelessness and the fact Ruth was not about to tell all, Naomi interjected, "Talk to me. Don't be coy with me, dear."

To which Ruth replied with a soft smile, "Well, I was once hoping for the kind of love you shared with Elliot...but I know that won't happen, so now I have settled for just raising my sons."

Startled, Naomi asked, "<u>Is there anything too hard for God</u>... huh, Ruth? Don't you believe that God can give you your heart's desire? Nothing is impossible with him, you know."

"I know he can," replied Ruth in an effort to defuse Naomi's Christian stance before the spotlight was turned to her commitment to living for God. "I entered those relationships hoping and praying that they'd last, while deep down inside I knew they were just pipe dreams…and besides, look at how old I am, and the time I have wasted on fruitless relationships."

Interrupting her flow of despair, Naomi commented, "God can also redeem the time, you know…and I won't call those relationships fruitless, if I were you. I am sure you know your sons are blessings. Those relationships were lessons you were supposed to learn from…and every day you are alive is an opportunity to make a change. You have to learn to forgive those in your past who have hurt you, despitefully used you, and even abused you. Most of all, you have to learn to forgive yourself. Don't let your past hinder your future, my dear. God is a God of forgiveness. Whenever you sincerely repent of your sins towards him; because of Jesus' sacrifice, God will look beyond your fault and see your need. He is a loving and merciful father.

"Also, Ruth, with love, you cannot enter a relationship thinking or hoping it will fail, because it will. Control your thoughts, my dear; control your thoughts. 'As a man thinketh in his heart, so is he'…through our thoughts we impregnate our future; and when we speak, we give birth. Don't be cynical about love…avoid the negative comments and attitudes. You see, Darling, what happens in your mind happens in time, so be careful. God will send the right person your way. When he comes, he will only be interested in giving and adding to your love, joy, peace, safety, happiness, and prosperity. If anyone comes around who subtracts from you instead of adding, I mean they leave you feeling drained and wondering if you've just given blood, he or she is not from the Lord. You are a very beautiful and attractive lady, Ruth. Don't give up on love…try dating again," Naomi said encouragingly.

"It's not that. Dating is not my problem…it's just that when things start getting serious, the men always end up walking away," Ruth replied, discouraged.

"So, let me get this straight," Naomi asked chuckling, "you can attract your Boaz, but you just can't keep him?"

"Don't laugh…that's sad," commented Ruth as she smiled in response, while silently wondering, *what the heck is Boaz?*

"That's the problem with you younger folks these days. You can attract your mates, but can't keep them," Naomi remarked, as her gaze wandered around the four corners of the ceiling checking for spider webs, a habit she had come to depend on as proof positive that a room was clean. "Okay, seriously, do you know what went wrong in each of those relationships…what you did wrong?"

Looking puzzled, Ruth defensively replied: "Me? I was always kind and faithful…I gave all my relationships everything I had…but those ungrateful dogs never seemed to appreciate it. At the onset, they act like they know they are being blessed by you; and the next thing you know, they start acting like it's their God-given right… and start taking you for granted. I may be a lot of things, but I'm no doormat."

Reflecting on Ruth's stance and of how she saw herself as being faultless in all these relationships, Naomi paused, then cynically remarked, "Our present is based on decisions we've made in the past. Do you walk on water, Honey? If so, please heal my hips and give me strength. If not, you need to start looking at what you did wrong on your part...forgiveness has nothing to do with consequences, my dear. God can forgive us, but it's the consequences of our past actions, quiet as they're kept, that we have to live with. Mind you, he gives us his grace and mercy to make the consequence manageable, but we still have to face the music. I have found out over the years that the most difficult person to forgive is oneself. We have to learn to forgive ourselves when we know we have sinned against God. We sometimes forget what we are fighting for, and find it easier to forgive others. But when the tide is turned, we cannot bring ourselves to go past the shame, guilt, and regrets of our indiscretions. For starters, you need to hold yourself accountable in every situation you find yourself. I mean accountable for your actions, words, feelings and thoughts. In this free society, no one can make you do things you don't want to do, say words that are not becoming of you, have feelings and thoughts of what's irrelevant to you. You also want to be clear in your communications with people. Always let people know who you are and what you stand for. If you can't tolerate 'X,' then let them know it before you regret it. What I have seen over the years is that a lot of people fail to draw their line in the sand early in their relationships. I mean both men and women. They try to impress their partners by setting standards they'll later find hard to maintain, and when it is expected of them, they retreat to the shadows in frustration. Don't let the moment set the pace. Set your boundaries early…don't wait until after he's come to expect certain patterns, then try to change up on him. That is a common mistake that goes unnoticed. I am glad I warned my Larry and Edwin about their expectations, early in life.

"Let me ask you this…what are your values, Ruth…what are your values? You see, our values control our behavior, and our behavior is the reflection of what we believe. You need to value authenticity because a relationship that is based on deceit is one that will not survive, Darling. Baby, contrary to popular belief, it is also possible to pray for and receive a blessing that you are not really ready for. The devil will give you options before the manifestation of a godly blessing, but as you know, the blessings of the Lord maketh rich and addeth no sorrow with it. Right? So you have to ask yourself, are my desires clouding my discernment, and is this from the Lord? Your answer will be there to guide you…but most times we just go with the first thing that comes along or the next best thing."

*Wow!* Ruth thought, as she reflected on her romantic periods. *She is so right.*

But time had crept up on them, and she had to report for duty. Rising from her chair, Ruth leaned over, gave Naomi a big hug in appreciation, thanked her friend, kissed her on the cheek, and whispered that she would be back during her break. The two ladies smiled as Ruth left the room. Naomi could tell that her friend was feeling relieved, and that brought joy to her heart.

Somehow, those words resonated in Ruth's mind. For once, she had an inkling of what she might have done wrong in her past, a trickle of the answer to her questions. This uplifted her spirit as she looked forward to sitting down with her sage, mentor and friend, Naomi.

Break time couldn't come fast enough for Ruth. She had replayed her earlier conversation with Naomi, over and over again in her mind, throughout the first half of her shift. *I must learn to control my thoughts, and not let the moment set the pace*, she kept on soliloquizing. During her break, Ruth had a quick bite and ran over to her darling Naomi, who was also excited at the breakthrough and waiting expectantly to see her friend.

"So tell me," Naomi started, as soon as Ruth walked into her room, "what's your flavor? I mean, what is your preference of the ideal mate for you?"

With a bashful smile, Ruth reached over to Naomi's toiletries, took out her brush and comb, and proceeded to comb her friend's silver hair as she described her ideal man.

"He should be standing at least six feet tall, rugged on the outside, your usual GQ muscular type, sensitive, kind, sincere, faithful, loves the outdoors, family-oriented, very intelligent, a giver, a good listener, a great cook…so that he can prepare lunch or dinner when I'm running late. Proactive, loves my sons, handsome, charismatic, financially secure, adores the ground I walk on…what else? What else? And, oh yeah, he must be a Christian."

Bursting out in laughter, Naomi exclaimed, "That's who I was looking for, before I met Elliot!" After calming down from her uncontrollable laughter and wiping the tears off her face, she said, "Over the years, I have come to realize that no one can find **all** they want in one person and still hold on to them…you see, that person will become an idol or your god…and our God is a jealous God… he doesn't share his love or his throne. Baby, <u>you cannot love anything or anyone else more than you love God</u>. For some people, it's their cars; some, their jobs; some, their homes; some, their children; some, their pets; some, their partners; some, their possessions and wealth; and some, even themselves. You cannot do that, don't make a god out of anyone or anything else…God is God, and God alone. God will never give you a life that makes him unnecessary, Ruth. You will have to need him and only him sometimes. Anyway, so tell me, have you considered Dr. Swift?"

"Well, he has asked me out a couple of times before, but I had to decline. I was scared of entering into another relationship…he was on the rebound from a messy divorce…and he is …um … a little short for me," Ruth recounted.

Dr. Swift was, in reality, not Ruth's flavor, even though he was a brilliant multi-disciplinary physician and surgeon, one of the most renowned providers in the medical profession, chairman of the GMNH board of directors, and a very wealthy man with a heart of gold. He stood at about two inches below her, wore those outdated coke bottle glasses, and was a little on the slim side.

Smiling, Naomi said: "Baby, don't be superficial, and go for the appearance…you of all people should know, appearance can change with time…or even a freak accident. You see, from your list of needs and wants, you have to prioritize the qualities that are absolutely important to you as a lady, and a mother. The catch is, if a man can meet those needs, he can work on some of those wants, if he is in love with you."

"Well, how do I know that he really loves me?" Ruth asked.

Smiling, she replied, "It's not in his kiss, my dear. If that were the case, every good kisser would be married. You have to ask your-self, 'Does he anticipate my needs?' Mind you, that does not mean that he buys everything for you, because if that's the case, only the rich will have partners. You can give without loving, but you can't love without giving. So, is he a giver? Does he give of him-self? Would he rather go without so you can have? You see, a man is a provider and a giver. For example, if he really loves you, the moment you maybe jokingly say you'd like to have something, until he satisfies that need or want, it quietly becomes a project to him. Does he speak highly of the women in his life, like his mother and sisters? Is he proud of you every day, every time, and everywhere? Or is it just around certain people, at certain times, in certain places? Don't let him pick the place, you pick the place. Is he excited by your presence? Do his eyes brighten up when he sees you? Does his voice come alive with joy when you are around? Does he feel down when you are not around? Is he still enamored by you even without having sex? How much does he know about you? Is he interested in knowing about you? Does he ask you about you and your life? And I don't mean the usual stuff, just to make small talk. To prove that he knows you and is really interested in you, quiz him on the things you have discussed with him about your life earlier in the relationship… and don't you even think about sleeping with someone who doesn't know you and respect you as a person. You would need to find out who he is as a man, and not just in his roles that he fulfills.

"By the way, what is this third date rule I hear you young folks talking about these days? I think it's ridiculous…it takes a lifetime to know someone, and yet most girls these days just give up their flower to a stranger, then get depressed when he walks away, leaving them with no regard as a person." Frustrated with the times, and how some younger women conducted their lives, Naomi became flustered as she continued: "People just jump from one partner to another with no respect for themselves…this generation can learn a lot from nature…take a look at the wild geese the next time they come around…they are partnered for life, you know."

Smiling to calm her friend down, Ruth got up from the chair, where Naomi's wisdom had left her spellbound, and kissed her on the cheek. She told Naomi that she had to return to work, and she would see her tomorrow if Naomi was asleep by the time she got off from work.

Naomi then remarked, "Give Dr. Swift another chance…he is a good man…he might be the one."

Smiling back at her friend, after kissing each other goodnight, Ruth left Naomi, and felt a lot better than she did when she came into work that day.

After work that night, Ruth stopped by Naomi's room, but she was fast asleep. Leaving GMNH on her way home to Brian and Marcus, Ruth could not help but think of all the wisdom she had gained from Naomi that day, from controlling her thoughts to the wild geese partnering for life. A smile overshadowed her face at the knowledge and wisdom Naomi possessed. Before settling down to sleep that night, Ruth walked over to the bookcase next to the computer in the family room, and grabbed one of the surplus notebooks she had bought for the boys at the start of the academic year. Determined to succeed at her next relationship, Ruth took the notebook upstairs and proceeded to write down all the wisdom she gained from Naomi that day.

"This will be my 'notebook,'" she thought out loud. "My 'wisdom journal.' I will make good use of every opportunity I have to learn from the wisdom of Naomi."

It was inspiring to her, and she thanked the Lord that night for putting Naomi in her life. After writing down the "day's wisdom" in her journal, Ruth jumped into bed, and soon fell asleep with thoughts of Dr. Swift's good qualities in her mind.

# The Invitation

*"Will opens the door to success, both brilliant and happy."*
*–Louis Pasteur*

Unlike the previous morning, Ruth woke up with a song of praise in her heart. She had a restful night, and was excited about continuing her conversation with Naomi. Before leaving home for work that day, Ruth called Naomi and asked if she could get her anything, as she was stopping by the grocery store before coming in to work. Naomi appreciated the offer and thanked Ruth, asking for the biggest and freshest looking bananas she could find. That, Ruth did. Arriving about forty-five minutes before her scheduled work time, Ruth walked over to her friend, greeted her with a hug and a kiss, put the bananas on the table, took out Naomi's comb and brush from the drawer, and proceeded to do her friend's hair. The two conversed about Naomi's day, and the effects of her medications. After doing her hair, with about fifteen minutes to spare, Ruth applied some lotion to Naomi's ashy feet, then proceeded to massage them for circulation. Naomi thanked her friend for her kindness, the two hugged and kissed, and Ruth departed for the start of her shift.

At her station, there was a note stating Dr. Swift had called a couple of times earlier. Coincidentally, shortly after she arrived, the phone rang and it was the doctor.

Sounding a little nervous, Dr. Swift said, "Ruth, um, I know I've asked you this before...but, um, I just thought I'd try again...I am not sure...um...of what your schedule is like, but if you won't mind...um, I mean if it's okay with you, would you mind having lunch with me sometime this week? I mean if it's okay with you... um...if you have time..."

Teasing the nervous fellow, who from the sound of his voice was clearly in awe of her, Ruth replied with a giggle, "Are you asking me out on a date, Dr. Swift?"

Stammering he replied "Um...um... yeah...if it's okay with you."

"Then I accept," she said. "How about tomorrow?"

"You choose the time and the place and I will even come pick you up, if it's okay with you," replied Dr. Swift, as he slowly regained his confidence.

Ruth chose a moderately conservative Italian restaurant and agreed to meet Dr. Swift at 12:30 for lunch the following day. After they hung up, she walked over to Naomi, who was all propped up in bed and smiling as if she overheard the conversation.

Ruth asked, "What did you say?"

Now beaming with a mischievous smile, "match-maker" Naomi burst into laughter as she retorted: "What? Why does everyone always assume that I said or did something when things are going well?"

Shaking her head, and with a wink of approval, Ruth said, "I will see you later," then returned back to her station, smiling.

During her break, the two ladies huddled up in Naomi's room in preparation for the next day's excitement.

"I haven't felt this much joy in a while!" Naomi exclaimed. "You'll see, he is a good man...and I think he is the one."

With a reserved smile, Ruth could not help but silently rehearse the notes from her "wisdom journal": *I need to control my thoughts.*

Beckoning to Ruth to pull her chair closer, with a serious look in her eyes, Naomi started stroking the back of Ruth's hand, and in a comforting voice, said, "I know this is a little frightening for you, my dear...but go in with the expectation that it will work. Life is not a game of chance. Don't hope for love; go for love. Make choices, don't take chances with your life. When you sit with a man...and I mean 'a man,' he may not say a lot, but listen carefully, because everything he says has meaning...don't think anything trivial of even his jokes...they can lead you to where he is. Don't fall for the smooth talker, and be careful of what you show him. From the Garden, we yield to what we hear, while men yield to what they see. That is why so many women are in abusive relationships. They discount the way they are being treated or what they see happening to them, and go by what they hear these men tell them. A man is hooked by what you show him. Why do you think so many girls today wear skimpy outfits? Subconsciously, they know the more they show, the more he'll want. You see, a man is a hunter, and he will seek what he's after, both non-physical and physical. So pay close attention to him. It's up to you to train him to seek you as an intellect, a spiritual being, a confidant, a friend, a helpmeet, and not an orgasm coolant or steam reliever. Dress conservatively while you are courting him…you will train his mind to start thinking of you as a person and not a sex object. Ruth, honey, whatever you do, never try to manipulate your partner with your love, okay? That is what will lead to conditional love, and that's not what God has called you to experience or give."

Along with the wisdom she had already shared, Naomi continued, "If there is something he is doing that you do not particularly care for, don't be afraid to let him know it immediately…again, draw your line in the sand. It's better for him to know it now, than for him to think it's alright, and then later on in the relationship, you flip out on him out of frustration. The only thing I'll caution you is that when you do try to change a behavior, be a lady about it, not a woman; choose your words carefully. You do not have to yell to be heard. Yes, you can outtalk him and out-argue him…but please, please don't raise your voice at him. Especially when in public. He is not your child…don't disrespect him. You will end up winning the battle, but losing the war."

While Naomi was busy talking, Ruth pondered these words of wisdom as her dazed mind flashed back to her previous relationships in which she had to yell, scream, force, and fight, just to make a point or get her way. With a slight tap on the wrist from Naomi, Ruth was brought back to the reality of going on her first date in a long while. It was a major decision she had just made. It could mean breaking her decision to be single for the rest of her life.

It could also lead to her sons being hurt again. *No, no, no, I must control my thoughts.* Ruth battled within. With all the wisdom she was absorbing that evening, she had little time to ask Naomi why she thought Dr. Swift would be "the one" before her break expired.

Excitedly, Ruth asked the elder lady, "Do tell me, when and how did you come to meet Dr. Swift?"

"Well," Naomi began, "he is actually a half-brother of my Elliot. Somehow Elliot's dad couldn't keep his pants on during his old age, and decided to try his luck with a younger woman when Elliot was in his late thirties. He has been close to me, and is also loved and respected by all the members of our family. As you know, he is also a brilliant physician…and between the two of us," she whispered, "let's say there are a lot of things he can afford and he has a very generous spirit."

"Hmm!" sighed Ruth as she got up from her seat, smiling. "I've got to get back to work…if you are still awake, I will give you a big goodnight hug, if not, I will tell you how I made out when I see you tomorrow." After they kissed each other on the cheeks, Ruth left

Naomi's room and went back to work. The night dragged on, but Ruth was once again excited about romance.

As usual, Naomi was fast asleep when Ruth stopped by to say goodnight, but that didn't dampen her spirit. When she got home that night, the boys were up waiting for her. After about forty-five minutes with her sons, she put them to bed, secured the house, went upstairs and headed straight for her bedroom. Ruth then decided to pack a duffle bag that she would take with her when she left the house the next day, to carry her uniform and other essentials. She wasn't sure of how long this lunch date would be, and the restaurant was about twenty minutes away from her home, but closer to GMNH.

*Tomorrow has to be different,* Ruth thought as she headed for her closet. *I want to make that man's glasses crack…* but then she remembered Naomi's advice: "Dress conservatively while you are courting him…you will train his mind to start thinking of you as a person, and not a sex object." *That's a bummer,* she thought, staring at her red ultra top, with slits at both sides that could stop traffic. Shifting her eyes to the left, she saw a navy blue dress that made her look absolutely breathtaking. *I am not going to church,* she argued within. *It's just a casual date. Okay, okay, what about this beige… no, what if I spill some soup or sauce on myself…no, bad idea… let's try this bottle green two piece, pants suit…no, too formal… hmm! Okay, I will just wear this cerulean blouse. It's fitted, but not too tight… sporty, not formal, and the three-quarter sleeves will let me be comfortable if it's too warm in the restaurant; it'll be perfect with these black fitted plaid pants…this is conservative enough,* thought Ruth, after about forty-five minutes of search. She took out her selection and carefully examined it to make sure that there were no loose threads, buttons, or broken zipper.

Satisfied, Ruth turned to her shoes. Lucky for her, she had a fairly new black tongue-style shoe with a stylish chunky heel and scallop detailing, Stanhope shoes that she had worn only once before. She felt they made her look somewhat sophisticated. She was all settled. Holding the outfit in front of herself at the mirror, Ruth smiled as her confidence yawned and stretched from its long nap. Before going to bed that night, after saying her prayers — which, not surprisingly, had a different tone and were more praise than petition — Ruth settled down to update her wisdom journal. She reflected on each wisdom pointer and added an application section on the opposite page for relevance.

*Oh, how I wish I knew then what I know now…I would have saved myself so much hurt and pain,* she reflected. Closing her journal and turning off the lights, with her bedroom door ajar so she could hear any strange sound in the house, and also see her sons' bedroom from her bed, Ruth settled down to sleep.

Sleep, however, was not forthcoming, as she thought of Naomi's words of wisdom and instructions, which sometimes came across as being harsh but were indeed enlightening. Ruth's mind also groped through the foggy alleys of her past, filled with faces, while looking for that lonely neon sign that still read "Open," an invitation to her last hurrah, as she wondered what a date with Dr. Swift would yield.

# The Date

*"The shortest and surest way to live with honor in the world is to be in reality what we appear to be." —Socrates*

The following day started off like most, but this time it was different. This time, Ruth had a quiet expectation she tried to suppress, a voice whispering that her life was about to change… it was her time to find true romance…it was her time to love and be loved…it was time to think before she leaped…and this time the man was unlike all the others she had been with in the past…he was a gentleman.

Like the promise of getting a new car after passing a driver's test, the waves of Ruth's excitement rolled into the shore of her reality as she hummed the chorus to her favorite religious song while getting dressed for her lunch date. *It would have been great to go on a date while I was out there looking for love…but after all these years when I have given up on love, here comes this opportunity with all the possibilities I could imagine. Why am I sweating?*

*I can't be nervous about this date…it's just a date!* **Ruth** reassured herself within as she wiped the sweat off her brow while transferring some necessary items from her regular bag to a nice, cute purse that complemented her outfit, before stepping in front of the mirror for a final overview. She saw a Ruth she'd never seen before. This time, Ruth looked mature, conservative, and drop-dead gorgeous… she was happy and confident…but most of all, she was a beautiful and attractive single mother, giving love another try. Grabbing the duffle bag, Ruth headed for the garage and put the bag in the trunk of her car. She then went into the house, made sure her home was secured, and then said a short prayer before heading off to the restaurant on her date.

Confident but somehow nervous, Ruth arrived at the restaurant at 12:25pm and was greeted and escorted over to their table by Dr. Swift, who had arrived a few minutes earlier and was waiting in the lobby area expectantly for Ruth. Like unwrapping a desired gift on Christmas day, his face beamed with delight at the sight of Ruth. Leaving the soft trail of her perfume as the couple was ushered to their table by the maitre d' through the aroma of the day's special, Ruth couldn't help but notice the proud look on Dr. Swift face when he guided her to her seat before taking his. This brought a gentle smile to Ruth's lips and she loved it. To break the ice, Dr. Swift insisted that she called him by his first name, Otis, and she reciprocated with Ruth. Other than the many compliments on her beauty that made Ruth blush with embarrassment while arming her confidence with love, the date was near perfect. They spoke about everything from the news, both local and international, to life at GMNH, to their Christian faith. Otis didn't waste much time, but made his intentions known to Ruth, when he declared:

"Umm, Ruth, I'm not sure if you've noticed that I'm a man of few words; and at this stage in my life I've come to realize that life is too short for me to be playing games or beating around the bush when it comes to important opportunities in my life. I'll just say it: I am in my early fifties, divorced, without children, and I am looking for someone with whom I can settle down and preferably have a child or two. I know this is just our first date, but at the same time, I truly care for you and can't hide it that I have feelings for you. I think you are a very beautiful lady…any man would be lucky to have you by his side."

*Whoa! That's a shocker.* Ruth thought; and after regaining her composure, she responded in a calm but firm voice: "Thank you…I am flattered. But I think we should take this a little slower and besides, we need to get to know each other a bit more before considering a long-term relationship…don't you think?"

"I do, I do. Trust me, I do," acknowledged Otis. "It's not that I want to rush you into anything we are both not prepared to handle; it's just that over the years, I have watched life pass me by while I was trying to play things safe because I was either shy or apprehensive of taking chances. This time, however, I am determined not to let the opportunity of getting to know you slip through my fingers."

Nodding to affirm Otis's rationale, Ruth gently smiled. Like the morning fog, a brief silence floated by the couple's table.

"Ruth, I'm sorry if I made you feel uncomfortable, I was just trying to lay my cards out on the table," Otis apologized. "Please forgive me. Would you?"

"Okay, no worries…I understand," Ruth conceded with a smile. "Now, since we are putting our cards out on the table, let me tell you a little about myself. I am a single mother with two sons: Brian, fourteen, and Marcus, eleven…their fathers are not in the picture. Although I am not planning on it, with the right partner I may be open to having more children; but I do not intend to go down that road again, alone," Ruth admitted.

In finding a common ground that would at least assure him a continuation of his stride towards being in a relationship with Ruth, Otis remarked: "In as much as I wouldn't mind having a child, a greater fact is that I would give that idea up if it means being without you. We don't have to have any more children…all I want is to be with you."

Smiling, Ruth asked: "Why me? Why do you like me?" There was a brief silence as Otis searched for the words to express the reasons that had him longing to be with Ruth.

"Where should I start?" Otis asked rhetorically. "Let me see… you are extremely beautiful to me; you are a good Christian lady; a wonderful mother; and from the way you are caring for Naomi, it shows that you are kind, respectful, considerate, and a lovely lady to have in my life."

This meant a lot to Ruth, and she gently smiled while masking the relief she felt in knowing that she had found a man who would still want to be with her even though she was a single mother who was well past her prime, with two kids for whom she cared.

With the pressure off, Otis extended Ruth an invitation to a second date, which she accepted. The lunch lasted for about an hour and a half. The food was delicious, and they shared some special moments in laughter. *Overall,* Ruth thought on her way over to the nursing home to bring Naomi up to speed, *I'd give this date 8.5 out of 10.*

Arriving at the GMNH all dressed up, Ruth walked up to Naomi, who was delighted and awestruck at Ruth's beauty. She knew Ruth was beautiful, but never imagined that her friend could look so stately. The two ladies hugged and impatiently, Naomi started in on discussing the date.

"So, so, how was it? Tell me, tell me everything, and don't leave out a single detail. I want to know everything." She shifted herself on the bed to get into a better position for the great narration.

Smiling, Ruth went down the whole sequence of events from her arriving at the restaurant, their meals, to her conversations with Otis. Naomi was a little disappointed at Otis's forwardness at discussing his intentions on their first date. She apologized to Ruth on his behalf and then proceeded to caution her on his statement about "doing anything to keep Ruth."

"You see, my dear, some people would say anything to get what they want in the moment…and then later they'd come to regret their decision and start looking for a way out. So you'd have to ask yourself," Naomi continued, "do I really want to have more children? If the answer, after careful thought, is no, let him know up front that you've given it a lot of thought and that you do not intend to have any more children. In that way, you will be offering him a way out before it gets too deep. If he still wants to go ahead with the relationship, then you have to remind him again to think seriously before a commitment is made. By commitment, I mean before he comes close to your rose. In short, honey, you have to make sure there are no loopholes in your relationship. That is what the period between courting, engaging, and getting married is supposed to satisfy. It was not intended as a period where you just sit down, twiddle your thumbs, go out on dates and make plans for the big day. It's true you cannot make him love you or make him stay, even after he has vowed 'till death do us part,' but if he is a man of integrity, he will live by his words. Do you understand, baby?"

Shaking her head in agreement, Ruth continued to describe Dr. Swift's character and demeanor to Naomi.

"He is such a caring person and a gentleman too…unlike the other men in my past…"

"Stop right there, Hon," Naomi quietly interrupted her. "<u>Please don't ever do that...don't compare the man you are with to others in your past, be it for good, or bad, no matter how innocent it feels or looks...especially to him. It could make him feel insecure, if a negative, or it could inflate his ego if a positive. This in turn, even though he won't say it, will make him see you as being privileged to be with him. That can affect the way he starts treating you. You see where I am going with this, darling? A man is a trailblazer...let him create his own path. You learn from your past, but every new relationship should be treated as a new book, not a new chapter. A chapter could be seen as a division of an existing framework, the continuation of a thought, sequence, or phase. A new book, on the other hand is a different story, a new beginning...do you get me, Hon?</u>"

This made so much sense to Ruth and she was appreciative of this time the two spent together. However, she needed to get changed for her shift. As she was about to get up from her seat to leave Naomi and head down to her car in the parking lot to retrieve her duffle bag, Naomi spoke again.

"You look so stunning. Wait! Grab my camera...I need a picture of you in this outfit...it's in the second drawer, dear...oh no, sorry it's over here on the top shelf." Naomi pointed to the other side of the bed.

Popping her head outside to see if there was someone in the hallway who could take their pictures, Ruth beckoned to a nurse who came running, thinking it was an emergency. She proceeded to take three stills of the two ladies, and a couple of singles of Ruth. Her shift started like any other and she was all changed into her nursing uniform on time, but for the hairstyle and makeup still intact from her lunch date. Ruth settled in her role as supervisor for the second shift.

Knowing that Ruth would have shared her experience on the date with Naomi, and being unsure of her perception of their date after his inappropriate declaration of his intentions, Dr. Swift called Naomi and enquired about his overall performance, to get feedback without asking Ruth directly. Though not excellent, it was an encouraging feedback and he was delighted at the way Naomi said Ruth cared for him.

Later that day, Ruth was doing her rounds with a visiting physician when she heard a bit of commotion coming from the nurse's station. Taking a couple of steps back from a patient's room to check out the source of this excitement, she peered down the hallway and saw a driver from a local florist, carrying the most gorgeous bouquet of roses. She immediately knew they were from Otis. Unsure of her feelings, heart pounding with pride mixed with anxiety and joy, her knees threatened to buckle as she walked gingerly towards the driver to receive her delivery before the whole nursing unit could be distracted. With tear-filled eyes, she signed for the roses and walked them straight into Naomi's room, set the vase on the table, and smiled as she returned back to work.

This was exciting. She had always envied other ladies in the past who received flowers from their loved ones. No one had ever been so kind to her, and for the first time in her entire adult life, Ruth felt like she was in a loving relationship, too.

Still full from lunch, Ruth decided to skip dinner and call Otis to thank him for the roses, before going over to Naomi's room. She called the cell number he had given her during their lunch date, which also happened to be his emergency contact number listed on the chart at the nursing station. In return, Ruth gave Otis her cell number and her house number, but insisted that he shouldn't call unless it was an emergency, as her sons also used the home phone. Expressing her sincere appreciation for the flowers, she told Otis that she would like to see him before their next date, which was scheduled for the following week. They agreed to meet for lunch at the same place that coming Friday.

Walking over to Naomi's room, Ruth felt like a woman in love, and she was happy about it. She told Naomi that this was the first bouquet of roses she had ever received, as the two ladies critically analyzed the beauty of Otis's gesture. There were three-dozen roses and they had the freshest and most tender petals imaginable. The fragrance hinted of romance in its purest form, with cheerful beads of water on some petals, as if rained on by love. The bouquet was made up of pink, white, yellow, and red roses in the most beautiful marble vase they'd ever seen, and on one of the stems was attached a note: "For every time I tried, a dozen roses was set aside," and signed, *OS.*

*This must have cost a fortune,* Ruth thought, as she and Naomi beamed in admiration.

Feeling uneasy, Ruth asked Naomi for her opinion on receiving the flowers at work.

"Oh, I see. You are trying to be half-pregnant here, I take it. You want to be romanced, but don't want your mate to be romantic, huh? Well, let me ask you this: do you like the feeling you had when you received it?" Naomi asked.

"Hmm! Yes and no," Ruth replied. "Even though I really love and appreciate the gesture and excitement that comes with it, I felt somehow uneasy about the attention and obvious distraction it brought to the nursing home staff."

"It's okay to feel that way. You are in charge of your staff and you want them to be productive, so it's obvious a distraction can be viewed as a negative. For the attention you got, since this is your first, you are probably feeling shy, although deep down inside you are excited at the world knowing that you are a woman in love. It's understandable."

"Well, should I tell him not to send any more flowers to my work?" Ruth asked.

"To thine own self be true, my dear…to thine own self. Don't live your life trying to please other people, baby. To thine own self be true," Naomi stated. "If he stops sending flowers to you at work, who would know that you are a woman in love at home... your sons? Do you think you would have got this same excitement and attention if it were only your two sons who saw it? If the excitement of your sons at home is all that matters to you, then tell him to stop sending flowers to you at work. The only thing you must know is that <u>contrary to popular belief, a man is a listener and a thinker. He processes his behavior and words based on the hand he is dealt... he is not a mind reader</u>. If a woman acts a certain way or says a certain thing, his future actions are based on what he has heard and what he has seen. So don't feel slighted if you request this of him today, and he hardly goes down the flowery path of life again. Do you know the lengths he went to, just to make this gesture? You see, Baby, <u>men are just as sensitive as we are. Society tries to teach them to mask their feelings, but they feel, too, you know. They cry and feel unappreciated too. That does not mean you have to put up with something you don't like...as I've mentioned before, you just have to let them know in a cordial tone, and as a lady, what you want and what you don't want. There is a time and place for everything. To get your man to do what you want, find the time, find the place, and find the way to say what you want to say; and he will listen and do as you desire. If I were you, I would wait until the second and third gestures are made. Men are usually creatures of habit...this will give you the frequency, and the magnitude of his gestures... then you can know what will irk you in the future, and what you'd</u>

<u>love to see happen again. It's all about your approach, Baby…it's all about your approach.</u>

"But before we go marrying you off to someone, let me ask you this: are you really ready for love, Ruth…are you?" Before Ruth could respond, Naomi continued, "I am asking you this question because a lot of people say they are, but really aren't. Some don't know how, and others are not prepared to receive 'true' love when it comes around. You cannot be in love and stay the same way you were before the individual came into your life. We usually find it unreasonable to make an adjustment in our lifestyle, but want others to change theirs for us. Some of us are even too selfish to invite someone else in our lives. This just signifies that it was lust, and not love. Love will always make you want to change your lifestyle to welcome and accommodate your partner. Selfishness plus lust always leaves a broken heart, my dear."

# DISCUSSION

1) Is it okay to give all you have in order to win love?

2) In our modern day society, should women make marriage proposals to men?

3) Would you agree that it is all about the approach in getting your significant other to do exactly as you desire? Give two examples that confirm your answer.

4) Will you consider it "settling" if there is no original attraction?

5) How would you know if you are ready for love?

# PART II

# LOVE'S RESPONSE

# Decision

*"An appeaser is one who feeds a crocodile, hoping it will eat him last."*
— *Winston Churchill*

L ater that evening, after returning to work, another issue surfaced in Ruth's mind.

*The roses...how should I explain this to the boys...they have never seen me bring flowers home before...how would they feel... should I tell them about Otis...is it too soon...what if old hurtful feelings resurface? Oh Lord, I don't want to hurt these boys, no, not again...should I just be open with them...how would Marcus feel? He somehow can sense when I am sad and always sits next to me to comfort me...he is a little more protective of me than Brian...oh gosh!...should I just leave the roses here in Naomi's room? But that won't tell well if Otis sees them here...he'll probably think I did not appreciate them...I can leave them at the nursing station...but then everyone will want to know my business...Oh, Lord!*

Bothered at the thought of making a choice between taking the roses home or leaving them at work, at the end of her shift, with

Naomi asleep, Ruth took the flowers to her car and headed home. As she drove, the feeling of not wanting to hurt her sons again grew stronger. The only decision that came to mind, one that would save everyone's feelings, was to find a dumpster and throw the flowers out. Pulling into a gas station, with tear-filled eyes, Ruth grabbed the vase with trembling hands, detached the note that came with the bouquet and put it in her purse, and took out a couple of red roses. She could not bring herself to throwing out the beautiful vase, so she poured the rest of the roses out into a trash can.

As she pulled away weeping, Ruth cried out loud, and in mumbling words she complained: "For...for the first time in my life... I've, I've got my own flowers...and now I have to throw them away...what's wrong with me?"

Still sobbing, Ruth pulled into the empty parking lot of a nearby church, as she couldn't go home to the boys looking so sad. Realizing that her blood pressure was probably elevated, Ruth reached in her purse, took out and swallowed a of couple tablets from a bottle of antihypertensive that she should have been taking regularly, but only did so whenever she sensed an increase in her blood pressure. After about twenty minutes of collecting herself and applying fresh makeup, Ruth proceeded home to Brian and Marcus, who were still up waiting for her. She gave each boy a rose that she had rescued from the bouquet, and explained to them that red symbolized love, that she loved them very much, and so she had to get them the rose.

After big hugs and kisses from her sons, Ruth went downstairs when the boys were in bed, brought in the vase from the car, rinsed it out, wiped it, took it upstairs to her bedroom, and hid the empty vase at the back of her closet. Before going to sleep, and after updating her wisdom journal, Ruth's conscience weighed so heavily on her mind that she decided to go down on her knees and pray for forgiveness. While praying and trying to justify her actions in her thoughts, Ruth fell asleep on her knees, only to wake up sore a couple of hours later. With an elbow cramp and sore knees, she crawled into bed and resolved in her mind to tell her sons about Otis before things got out of hand.

Morning came too soon for Ruth. After sending the boys off to school, she went back upstairs to her bedroom, turned the TV on and decided to get some sleep before leaving for work. Falling in and out of sleep as the programs shifted from commercials and back on the TV, Ruth finally decided to rise and get her day started by calling Naomi to see how her morning was going. Naomi was appreciative of Ruth's call, and before the ladies got off the phone, Ruth asked her if she thought it was a good idea to tell Brian and Marcus about Otis.

"No, Baby!" Naomi exclaimed. "It's just a first date…give yourself some time…you will know when the time is right. I know the boys are also looking forward to a father figure in their lives…but give yourself some time. Be careful how you introduce a man into your life...they all say they are ready, but most are not. The fickle ones will shy away...but a 'mature man' will want to step up and take his place. You see, Baby, a man is a protector...but you should want to get to know who is protecting you and your family, won't you?" Then her voice dropped to a whisper. "I can hear Otis in the other room. He will be stopping by shortly to check up on me. Think about it, and we'll continue our conversation later, I will see you when you get in okay, Darling?"

Ruth couldn't spend much time with Naomi that afternoon, as she was running late for work. During her break period, she had to run to the store to pick up a few things the boys needed for school. Popping in to see her friend three to five minutes here and there during her shift, the two ladies briefly had time to discuss Ruth's next date with Otis the following day. The ladies kept their smiles as the hours went by without having their intimate conversations, even though Naomi was a little disappointed at the fact that she didn't get to spend as much time as she would have preferred with her adopted daughter and friend.

After putting the boys to sleep that night, Ruth headed for her closet to pick out her second date's outfit. She liked the compliments she received on her outfit the other day.

*If it is that easy to impress my admirers,* Ruth thought, *then definitely I could work out some more two-piece combinations with blouse and pants.* She preferred such outfits to skirts because of her figure. Ruth looked great in pants. This time she selected a figure-flattering white and blue belted blouse and navy blue pants, all the while thinking that she would spend more time talking to Otis this time around, than eating.

# Romance

*"Subdue your appetites, my dears, and you've conquered human nature." – Charles Dickens*

R uth's second date with Otis was more pleasant than the first, as they both felt more relaxed with each other. The formalities and pressures of a first date no longer caused anxiety for the couple. This time, Ruth set the pace. She didn't let her emotions or desire to get married someday rush her into discussing issues that would reveal her innermost being. She stopped, thought, and listened to every word that came out of Otis's mouth, and silently she thanked Naomi for the wisdom she had gleaned from her.

*I am doing fine,* thought Ruth proudly, *I am doing just fine.* In the past, she would have asked revealing questions that would lead to her reciprocating, and before long, her partner would know what turned her on, her sexual preferences, and most intimate secrets. But this time it was different. This time Ruth was proud of herself for being mature and acting as a lady should. Her conversations with Otis were surprisingly very pleasant, and not of a sexual nature or connotation. It was a clean, adult conversation, the type she wouldn't mind repeating to Naomi, who was now fast becoming her measuring rod for comportment.

Ruth had long ago caught Otis's attention, and he was now smitten by her. He thought very highly of her and was proud of her. Even more so than the first brand new Mercedes Benz he bought, Otis wanted to show off his trophy, Ruth, to the world, but had to control his emotions, as he didn't want to rush things and burn this bridge. The two shared a pleasant time, and after lunch, before leaving for work, they shared a hug and Otis kissed Ruth on the cheek. He really wanted to reach for her lips, but was cautious. Something Ruth appreciated.

Back at the GMNH, Naomi was given a rundown, and she was proud of her "daughter." Over the past few weeks, she could see the transformation that had taken place in Ruth's life and she was happy to know that her words did not go unheeded. Over the next couple of months, Ruth and Otis got to spend more time with each other over the phone. They met at least once a week for lunch. Otis sent flowers over to Ruth every other week at the nursing home, before Ruth explained that she would rather receive them once a quarter, to keep the anticipation alive and reduce Otis's expenses. She talked Otis into visiting an optometrist and changing his glasses to a much trendier frame, and as a result, Otis had been getting some welcome and un-welcomed attention from family, friends, coworkers, and even some strangers. With all this attraction, Ruth mentioned to Naomi that she had asked Otis to change his glasses and now she felt he was getting some un-welcome attention from the ladies, which didn't sit too well with her.

To this, Naomi responded: "Does he love you? Do you know that he loves you? If yes, then trust him to do the right thing. If he is one of those 'forgetful' ones, he would show his true color, and its then up to you to head out the door. If on the other hand he is a God-send, he will do right by you. You don't have to worry about love, my dear. You know 'the blessing of the Lord maketh rich, and he addeth no sorrow with it.' If you have to lose sleep and fight for his love, this relationship most likely isn't ordained by God. Yes, you'll have to take a stand to protect your blessing, because 'the enemy comes to kill, steal, and destroy,' but baby…not to the point where there is no peace of mind. That's why you have a God. And besides, be careful how you try to change someone else…you could end up opening the door to unwanted evil. With every change comes a new attitude, positive or negative…that is why trust is the primary key in any relationship. You want to also note, my dear, that there will come a time in each of your lives that you would notice a change… people change; it's a part of life. As we grow older, we tend to pull towards a familiar comfort. This comfort may not be familiar to your mate, but it's something you trust. It's not always for the bad, but be on your guard and keep your expectations in check, Sweetie…it's up to you to guide your partner into what is acceptable for you as changes present themselves, okay?"

Naomi and Ruth grew closer together as friends. Ruth now considered Naomi her best friend, and this feeling was reciprocated. One afternoon, after lunch, Ruth asked Otis to take a walk with her in the park, as it was a gorgeous day. They each had a pair of sneakers in their trunks, and the two had a nice romantic walk. This was really neat for Otis, because he had never walked aimlessly before, not even when he was dating while in medical school. This was not something Ruth was used to either, as she had worked tirelessly for most of her adult life. It was a moment that brought them closer, a moment that they would forever cherish.

When they walked back to their cars, Otis stopped and asked Ruth in a gentle and humble voice, "Can I kiss you?"

Smiling, she replied, "I thought you'd never ask."

It was a warm and passionate kiss, and they were both pleasantly surprised at how well the other could kiss. It was something worth looking forward to, and worth waiting for. Otis wanted to continue having these romantic moments, and invited Ruth to dinners and even some concerts, but she had to slow things down because this would mean taking time out from work; or spending less time with the boys. She explained this to him and he was willing to wait. Ruth had found the love of her life, and was beginning to believe what Naomi meant, when she said, "…he is the one."

When Ruth got back to work on the afternoon of her first romantic kiss with Otis, she wanted to share this moment with Naomi, but felt that it was best that some things were left unspoken. However, while visiting Naomi during her break, Ruth ventured to ask, "What if we wait all this time and then after we've settled down, we find out that the sex is not that great?"

With a curious look, as if in disbelief at her friend's audacity to ask about sex, Naomi softly responded, "Sex is an integral part of a relationship; but should not be the basis for your relationship, my dear. There's always someone else who can do it better than the next man can. That does not mean you should give up on the love you have, and go chasing the mirage of sex. He may not be the biggest, but as long as he treats you right and gets you there, stay on board… don't let sexual pleasures erase your blessings, Hon. I have seen too many people go after sex and end up being miserable. Yes, he can rock your world and make your pupils dilate, but there's always someone else better than him, and it goes the same way for men, too. You can teach someone how to have sexual pleasure, but you can't teach him or her how to be a good husband or wife if he or she doesn't really love you. Seek love, Honey, not sex. Disappointment in sex can be fixed, but disappointment in love is a totally different story. Don't worry, I can tell sex won't be your McGuffin."

*Mac-What?* Ruth thought. *Anyway, she does make a lot of sense.*

# The Approval

*"Everything in this world depends upon will."* – Benjamin Disraeli

A rriving at home one Friday night after work, with the boys still waiting up for her, Ruth was faced with the inevitable. After she read the boys their passage of scripture, Brian got up from his bed, walked over to Ruth, hugged her and told her that he was happy that she was happy.

Marcus also took the cue, got up and said, "Me too, Mom."

Wanting to seize this moment, Ruth sat the boys down on the bed, knelt down in front of them and proceeded to tell the boys that there was a wonderful man, a doctor at work, who was now her friend, and that she wanted the boys to meet him someday, if it was okay with them.

Shrugging his shoulder, Marcus asked, "Is he the one that's making you happy?" Smiling he continued. "Well if he promises to continue to make you happy, then sure, I am all for meeting him."

Brian was indifferent and asked, "What is his name...have we met him before?"

Ruth replied that her friend's name was Dr. Swift, and that she didn't believe the boys had met him when they visited the nursing home. There was a brief silence, then Ruth continued, "Are you sure it's okay with you? Let me know now, so that I can let him know... you guys know how much I love you, right? So if you don't want another man in our lives, just let me know and I will make sure he stops being my friend."

This was a tall order for the boys, seeing how much happier their mom was, but they gave Ruth the thumbs up, as each said, "I am okay with meeting him, Mom." Then they kissed her goodnight and jumped back into bed.

*Whew!* Ruth sighed as she walked back downstairs to secure her home after putting the boys to sleep. She was so relieved to gain the approval of her sons. They meant everything to her, and she wouldn't in any way whatsoever want to hurt them again. But this time, she knew it was different. Otis was a gentleman, and she was prepared to do all she could to make this work, if not for anything else but for the boys. Ruth was so excited that as soon as she had secured her home, she hastily updated her wisdom journal with lessons from Naomi, went down on her knees, said her prayers, and jumped into bed to call Otis.

This was a pleasant surprise for him, since he was not expecting to hear from Ruth that late in the night. The latest they had ever spoken was around 11pm, before she left work after her shift. This was a turn for the better in their relationship, and he could sense it in her voice. Otis was falling deeper in love with Ruth, and his world revolved around hers. Ruth had asked Otis about his schedule for the upcoming Saturday, and whether he would mind coming over to her home to meet her sons; and maybe they could even go out to eat, if that was okay with him. Her treat, she insisted.

Otis in turn was excited at the opportunity, and only a medical emergency would have kept him away.

# Drama

*"The ultimate measure of a man is not where he stands in moments of comfort and convenience, but where he stands at times of challenge and controversy." — Martin Luther King, Jr.*

That Saturday, Ruth called Naomi in the morning to let her know she had discussed her friendship with Otis, with the boys, and that he was coming over to meet them.

"Oh good," replied Naomi. "And how did they take it?"

"I will say, well," Ruth replied.

"Don't forget, my dear, just be careful on how you let Otis interact with the boys. <u>It takes time, so let time work it out. There are many more sunny days to come, many more family times to enjoy, so don't try to make up for lost time all at once.</u>"

Early that afternoon, Otis stopped by. As nervous as she had ever been, Ruth had to face the love of her life and her sons together. Hearing the doorbell ring, Ruth rushed towards the door so that she would be the one to greet Otis, and avoid any awkward moment in introducing him to the boys. With her heart beating faster as she approached the door, Ruth closed her eyes, took a couple of deep breaths to calm her nerves, and then opened the door to her home and invited Otis in with a handshake. The boys were already halfway across the living room, and so Ruth turned around and introduced the two parties vying for her heart to each other.

"Otis, I would like you to meet my sons, Brian and Marcus." Ruth pointed to the boys with an uncomfortable smile across her lips while the men greeted each other with firm handshakes.

"How are you guys doing?" Otis asked. "I've heard so many nice things about you...your Mom always talks about you and of how well you are doing in school."

"Thank you, and nice meeting you," Brian replied, as the boys gently nodded while excusing themselves from the living room. Offering Otis a chair, Ruth closed the door behind her. She gave him a questioning look, to evoke a response from Otis about his first impression of her sons. Otis smiled and reassured her.

"Fine young men. You've done a great job in raising your sons."

"I think so too, thank you," Ruth acknowledged.

While Otis and Ruth were in the living room talking, the boys took turns to peep out the window at Otis's BMW. Otis was most impressed with the knowledge of cars and intelligence of the boys as their conversations were overhead in the living room. They would have gone out for lunch, but then Ruth remembered Naomi's caution. But before she could quench the expectation she had built up in

Otis the night before, the doorbell rang, and they had an unexpected guest. It was Duncan, Marcus's dad.

He had moved back east, still nonchalant as ever before, tracked down Ruth and his son through an extended relative of Ruth, and then of all days, decided to visit unannounced.

The timing couldn't be more wrong for Ruth. This type of drama was what kept her from being in some past relationships, and now she faced one that threatened her future with Otis. The sound of his voice and the sight of this man brought back memories of abuse and pain, dejection, and despair; memories Ruth had buried deep within the hollow confines of her heart. As anger slowly burned the core of her soul, Ruth hastily walked towards the door, and opening it she asked, "What do you want?"

"Where's the love, girl? Where's the love?" Duncan replied. Time had taken its toll on Duncan. The once tall and handsome man for whose attention some ladies had dared to fight now featured gray hairs, sharp facial wrinkles, and a pot belly. He was drunk again. "Hey, can I at least come in?" he continued. "Well, at least let me see my son."

"You're not welcome here, and if you don't leave *now*, I will call the cops!" Ruth bellowed, in a tone that would have unnerved even Hannibal Lector.

This, however, did not dissuade Duncan as he got louder and verbally abusive in his demands to see his son.

The tension in the air was becoming stronger and sharper than a Samurai sword, so Otis stepped in and asked Ruth if she needed his help in handling the situation. Shaking in anger, Ruth slammed the door on Duncan, who continued to drunkenly ask for his son. Then she apologized to Otis for the scene and picked up the phone to call the cops.

After their early encounters with the law stemming from Ruth filing a complaint against him for theft and abuse, she had secured a restraining order on Duncan, which unfortunately had expired over the years. This was a very uncomfortable situation for Otis and the boys. Neither Brian nor Marcus ever knew their fathers. When the boys were younger, Ruth had shown the boys pictures of their dads, but Duncan was not recognizable to even his son. Ruth had attempted to explain to the boys that their respective dads had walked away from them and that she was the one who loved them the most. Both Brian and Marcus, who were very protective of their mother, were becoming very angry at this man bent on making their mom upset. The cops showed up shortly after. A scuffle ensued and after Duncan hit one of the officers, they forcibly removed him from the premises and escorted him to jail. Seeing how greatly uncomfortable the whole situation was, and how upset Ruth was, Otis asked if they would want to leave and go somewhere, to ease her mind and that of the boys.

Ruth understood how difficult this must be for Otis, so she once again apologized and asked if he could leave, and they would talk about it later. Otis didn't want to walk out on them at this difficult time, but knew it was best for Ruth, since she needed to explain what just happened to the boys. Before leaving, Otis hugged both boys and Ruth, and pleaded for them to call, if they needed him. It was a comforting and reassuring hug, one that let Ruth and her sons know they were not alone. And they appreciated it.

Accompanied by his thoughts while driving home, Otis battled within: *what will I be getting myself into? It is one thing to be in a relationship with someone who has some baggage, but dealing with a violent ex could be a very dangerous chance to take for love. But she loves me and I know she is not going back to her ex; so I am not threatened by him. But what about her son…what if he wants his dad in his life; how long do I have to put up with this drunken beef for the sake of Ruth's love? What if the other ex shows up and is also belligerent? Hmm! But my ex was violent too; and there was no stopping in her…I wonder what she is up to now. Hmm! The shoe could easily have been on the other foot. I will not hold this against Ruth after all, we all have a past. I only wish she would have let me stay to see them through this challenge…but I guess she felt just as uncomfortable as I did. I hope she doesn't turn me away because she thinks it's too much drama for me to go through. I cannot walk away from Ruth and her sons…that won't say much of me if I walk away from the love of my life when she finds herself in a difficult position.*

*I only wish Ruth could let me into her world so that I can be there for them.*

After Otis left, Ruth locked the door, turned the alarm on, and took the boys over to the kitchen table, where she sat them down and proceeded to tell them about the man who was just outside, making a scene. In tears, she explained that that was Duncan, Marcus's dad, and how much he had hurt her after Marcus was born. How she had to take out a restraining order on him because he was abusing her, and threatening their lives (while deliberately leaving out the part that he stole from them, to protect Marcus's feelings). Duncan never once supported her and her son, not with so much as a dime, and now he was threatening their peace again. She explained that she suspected this day would come, when either Duncan or Hamed, Brian's dad, would show up, wanting to be with their sons, but that she hadn't thought it would come at such an inopportune time. She then tabled the question and asked the boys if they wanted to see their dads and wanted them in their lives. She said she would let them think about it, and asked them to let her know, because she wouldn't stop them from seeing their dads, but she sure would not allow these men to mess up her life again. Without a second to spare, the boys expressed to their mom that they did not want these men or anyone who would make them upset in their lives.

As she spoke, the boys grew angry at the thought of someone hurting their mother this much. They had never seen their mom this upset, not even when she was feeling down, and in tears. This much rage and anger was never felt in their home before, and both Brian and Marcus did not want anything to do with these men. At this resolve, Ruth called the police station and asked if she could file for another restraining order against Duncan.

The clerk at the desk, hearing the uneasiness in her voice over the phone, told Ruth to come in and that he would assist her in the process. Ruth straightaway took the boys and headed for the station. She filed a permanent restraining order, and was told to send copies to the boys' school and other establishments they frequented.

Later that evening, when the boys were in their room, Ruth lay across her bed. With a pounding headache from the stress of the day, she sobbed bitterly, quietly asking, "Why me? Of all the times in my life, why now, why did this have to happen to me just when I am trying to move on, and nurture a new relationship, with a man who could possibly be the love of my life?"

# Eclipse

*"Dost thou love life? Then do not squander time; for that's*
*the stuff that life is made of."*
*— Benjamin Franklin*

O tis, who had been calling periodically throughout the day to check on his love, called early that evening to comfort her. Ruth told him that she had gone down to the station to file for a restraining order, and that she was sorry for everything that transpired that day.

"I may not know what you are going through," Otis said, "but I went through something that battered my faith in love, with my ex. I had to get a restraining order on this woman, too. She was so cruel and ruthless that I swore to myself I would never let another person close to my heart. Not until I saw you, when I started working at the nursing home. Honey, I am with you and we will go through this together."

It was like a burden had been lifted off her shoulders...these words were so comforting to Ruth. For once in her life she had a

"Man." Someone who would not shy away from responsibilities; and one who would be by her side through the good times and the bad. Finally, Ruth knew she was loved. To put the icing on the cake, Otis asked if he could accompany them to church on Sunday, as he just wanted to be around her and the boys. This blew the lid off of Ruth's love reservoir, and he plunged right into her heart.

*Wow,* she thought, *I can't even get my sons to come to church with me, sometimes, and here is this loving man who is actually volunteering to go to church with me, just to be close to us. Wow!*

She sighed. Ruth agreed and after fifteen minutes of expressing her appreciation and Otis's reassurance of his commitment, they decided to call it a night and get some rest. Otis would be picking up her and the boys up around 7:30am, in time for the 8:00am morning worship service. Ruth and the boys usually attended church that early so they could have the rest of the day to hang out and get ready for the coming week. Feeling a lot better from her conversation with Otis, Ruth picked herself up from the bed, headed over to the boys' room, and crawled unto their bed under the covers between them. She told the boys Otis would be joining them, and then the three of them took turns at telling jokes until they fell asleep with the lights on.

Waking up at about 1:30am, she quietly got up, turned the light off, left her sons, and stumbled back over to her room, where she said her prayers and crawled unto her bed.

The alarm went off at 5:00am. Ruth got up, took her shower, and started getting ready for church. This Sunday would be unlike any other Sunday she'd had to endure before in church. This time, she would have a man by her side, and not a relative or coworker she'd invited to family and friends day at the church. This time, she could show the world that she was loveable and in a loving relationship with a man who was not just any other man. Her man was a doctor, a kind and caring one, a responsible and handsome Christian man, who was also in love with her. Ruth was excited about attending service with the men in her life. She felt vindicated by God for all her tears and lonely years. She was thankful to God for Naomi, and sending Otis into her life.

She woke the boys up at 6:00am and told them to hurry up and get ready for service, as Otis would be on his way over. Ruth was so elegantly dressed in a turquoise-blue outfit, with her hair pulled back and rolled in a Victorian style, that the boys had to comment on her beauty. Brian and Marcus, of course, were neatly dressed in suits; a practice Ruth had cultivated in them, explaining that the first impression went a long way. One could never have a second chance to make a first impression, so dressing properly was always a priority to the boys if they didn't want their mom to be disappointed with them. They were all dressed and ready to go around 7am. Wanting to make up for the treat she missed, thanks to Duncan that Saturday, she gave the boys a light breakfast, and told them they would go out after service.

Otis, prompt as always, was there at 7:20am. They invited him in for a quick prayer, and then the four of them headed off to church in Otis's BMW. The church was about twenty minutes away, and the boys enjoyed the ride as they admired the comfort of the car and the gizmos it contained, unlike Ruth's five-year-old Ford Explorer. It wasn't a bad ride either, but just not a BMW 760Li.

Arriving at the church, the boys got out of the car and opened the door for Ruth before Otis could get to her side. He was impressed. Ruth had taken the time to teach the boys some etiquette and being gentlemen, and they were the better for it. Ruth felt high and lifted up. She had never felt this way before, happy to be alive, happy to have her sons walking in front of her, and most importantly, happy to be in love.

Otis had complimented her all the way to the church and couldn't keep his eyes off of her. He was in awe of Ruth, and loving her more and more as the minutes rolled by.

During the service, Ruth could feel the piercing eyes of some members of the congregation all over her, checking out her outfit, admiring how beautiful she looked, both men and women. She even caught some of her "Christian" sisters (married, single, and divorced) checking out her man...and she was proud. The sermon that morning just flew in one of Ruth's ears and out the other. Even Brian and Marcus felt good. All Otis could see was Ruth.

*Wow! How blessed am I,* he thought.

After service, Ruth took the time to introduce Otis to the pastor and some church mothers, who were being a little too intrusive for Ruth. She was the envy of the day — an acknowledgment that, not surprisingly, some members of the church didn't share. Leaving church, she kindly asked Otis if he would mind going out to breakfast with her and the boys, and stated that it was her treat since she missed her chance the day before.

When Otis agreed to breakfast, the four of them headed for a trendy restaurant, close to their home but some thirty minutes away from the church that offered Sunday breakfast buffet. As they ate, looking at the boys from across the table, Ruth saw happiness in their faces; something that had long been missing from their lives. She was at peace, with Otis by her side.

After the boys got up for a second helping, Ruth reached over to Otis and gave him a very warm and passionate kiss on the lips. She said "Thank you," as she wiped the lipstick from his lips.

Surprise at his good fortune lit up his eyes. Blushing, Otis asked, "What was that for?"

"For being who you are," Ruth replied and smiled.

Breakfast lasted for about an hour and a half, and then Otis drove Ruth and her sons back home. Brian and Marcus had taken a liking to Otis, and were now striking up conversations with him about his car and his job. They thought he was a really nice man, and respected him.

Ruth was happy when they arrived home. She asked Otis to come in and they said a prayer of thanksgiving for the service, breakfast, and for each other's lives. Ruth didn't want him to leave, but knew it would be too much of her to ask him to stay. Otis gave the boys a hug, then Ruth walked him to the door, where she gave him a quick hug and peck on the cheek while the boys peeped out the window to take one last look at the car. Unable to bear the urge, Ruth asked Otis if he'd like to stay. He thanked her, but said he had to get home and make some notes for work that Monday. Ruth was disappointed, but couldn't stop him, and tried not to reveal her feelings.

After Otis left, Ruth couldn't wait to talk to Naomi and bring her up to speed on the weekend's events. She needed someone to talk to, someone with whom she could share her joys. She reached out for Naomi, but she had visitors. Her sons and their families were there, so the two ladies agreed to talk later that evening. Ruth and her sons were full from breakfast, so after changing into their casual wear, they lounged around, while slowly accomplishing their Sunday chores in preparation for the coming week.

Later that day, as the three of them settled down to watch a movie, Ruth asked the boys, "So what do you think...what do you think of Dr. Swift...do you like him?"

"Yeah, Mom, I think he's cool," was the overwhelming affirmation. This was good enough for Ruth, and she agreed, "I think so, too."

Still feeling a little disappointed at Otis not wanting to stay a while after service, Ruth stared at the TV as her thoughts reached for straws to justify his wanting to leave. *Maybe he was tired of us. Maybe it's all too overwhelming. Maybe I came on too strong with that kiss. Maybe he had to go meet someone else. Maybe he was just tired and wanted to rest…after all, breakfast was filling…but he could have rested here…who makes notes anyway on a beautiful Sunday afternoon? Maybe what happened yesterday with Duncan made him uncomfortable at my place. Maybe it's the boys…no that can't be, he loves children, and knows how much my sons mean to me.*

The thoughts became so upsetting for Ruth that she had to take a deep breath and try to focus on the movie they were watching. It was hard for her, but then she remembered Naomi's advice to control her thoughts. "As a man thinketh in his heart, so is he…through our thoughts we impregnate our future, and when we speak, we give birth. Don't be cynical about love, Hon…avoid the negative comments and attitudes."

At about 4pm, Otis called and asked if she and the boys would like to go for a Sunday drive. He explained that he had finished his notes and was already missing their company. Ruth gracefully turned him down, asked for a rain check and explained that she was still working on preparing the boys for school the coming week.

Sensing that his darling was a little cold on the phone, Otis asked if everything was all right, and if there was anything she wanted to talk about, but Ruth said she was fine, but that she was busy getting the boys were ready for school.

Agreeing to call him when she was settled, Ruth got off the phone, walked into her bedroom, closed the door behind her, sat on the bed, then grabbed a pillow and buried her face in it as she screamed, "Urghh! What is wrong with me...why do I have to lie... why am I so mean?...Urghh!" Disgusted with herself, she quietly asked God to forgive her and promised she would do better, if only he could give her another opportunity. After collecting herself, Ruth went back and joined her sons as she tried to watch the remaining quarter of the movie.

Feeling guilty about the way she treated Otis, Ruth called him around 5pm and asked if he was still up for a ride. Poor Otis was already in his pajamas, as he had already called it a night, without any plans for the rest of the day. Excited about being around Ruth again, he agreed, freshened up, got dressed and headed over to Ruth's.

Brian and Marcus were excited. They always appreciated whatever opportunity they had to go out, especially in a BMW. When Otis picked them up, they first went for some ice cream, then cruised up the highway to nowhere. The mood was lively. They joked, laughed, and enjoyed the scenery as the sun took a bow at the curtain call. This was just like Ruth had always imagined her family would be. She loved it and enjoyed the time they spent together.

After an hour up the interstate highway, they decided to turn around and head back, to get the boys home before it was too late. Otis was happy, too. He loved Ruth and cherished every moment they spend together.

"Oh no!" Ruth exclaimed. "I've probably missed Naomi's call."

In response, Otis noted with a smile, "She'll probably guess you are with me."

After they got back home, Ruth invited Otis in and asked if he'd mind joining them for dinner. Anything to make him stay longer. Otis agreed and he settled in the living room with the boys. They walked him through their impressive collection of DVDs and video games while Ruth prepared dinner for her men. The boys took turns at helping her out with setting the table, as she consciously tried to make the best impression on Otis. Her cooking had to be exquisite, and their table manners should be impeccable. She wanted so badly to show Otis that she could be as much a wife and a mother as she was beautiful.

She didn't have to work too hard on this one, though. He was sold from the morning service.

# Threshold

*"There hath no temptation taken you but such as is common to man: but God is faithful who will not suffer you to be tempted above that ye are able; but with the temptation also make a way of escape that ye may be able to bear it"…(1 Corinthians 10:13)*

After dinner, which Otis didn't eat much of since he had had some cookies shortly before going on the Sunday drive, during which he also had some ice cream, he asked if he could help out with the dishes, clearing the table or something. But Brian and Marcus pointed both him and Ruth to the living room, saying he was the guest and they would take care of it. Ruth was disappointed that Otis didn't eat all his food, but was also happy that she was left alone with her man. She knew that this could only get better if she played her cards right, and that was her goal. This time, she would do her best to make it work. She thought about apologizing to Otis for turning him down earlier, but decided it was best to let sleeping dogs lie.

Still a little concerned about the chill he experienced during their earlier conversation on the phone, Otis asked if everything was okay with Ruth, and if she was upset about anything earlier. She said no, she was just a little tired, but apologized if she was a little abrupt. She handed Otis the TV's remote control, and the two sat next to each other on the sofa as he surfed the channels for something they would all enjoy.

"What would you like to watch?" Otis asked.

Ruth was tempted to say her favorite channels were only available in her bedroom, but remembered Naomi's advice that she had to be a lady and train Otis's mind to start thinking of her as a person and not a sex object.

This was boring for her too, but she said, "Let's go to CNN. I haven't watched the news today."

After cleaning up, the boys came back into the living room, and Ruth briefly left to call Naomi and apologize for not having enough time to talk to her that evening. She explained that Otis was over and so she would stop by before work the following day.

Before getting off the phone, Naomi cautioned her, "<u>Don't let him stay too long. Remember, you are a lady, and a mother.</u>"

Running back to her men, Ruth told the boys to say goodnight to Dr. Swift and go prepare for bed. Obeying, the boys said goodnight and headed off to their room as Ruth settled down on the sofa next to Otis. She sat so close that her breast actually touched the side of his arm. She was feeling for him, but knew it would be wrong and risky to go any further, on her part, if she valued this relationship. Leaning over, Ruth grabbed the back of his neck, held him close to her breast, and kissed him passionately. It was a long kiss, but then she had to stop, for she could hear Naomi's voice so clearly in her head. It was the kind of penetrating voice that troubled the mind when she went against its will. She had to stop. Taking a deep breath, Ruth apologized to Otis and said that she'd have to call it a night, as she had to go put the boys to sleep.

He didn't want to stop, either. With spurts of broken kisses that yearned for more, she begged him to stop, while reaching in passion for one last kiss that led to yet another. Ruth finally got up, wiped her face with the palms of her hands, and reached out to Otis to bring him to his feet. Smiling, they both agreed that it was best to take things slow and show some restraint at this point in their relationship. Being a gentleman, Otis got up and then gave Ruth a hug.

Not wanting to turn the outside light on, she walked him outside and closed the door behind them. The two then hugged and kissed each other passionately again, and this time it was more intense. Ruth found herself yielding to her impulses as her hand fell and reached out for Otis's zipper to feel his weight. She had temporarily succeeded in blocking out the still small voice that repeated Naomi's wisdom.

She was shocked when Otis paused, backed up and said, "Honey, you know I want you, and everything in me is crying out for you, but do we want to go down this path and possibly hinder our blessing?"

This was a shocker for Ruth. She had never been rejected when it came to sex before, and here this man had just proved that not all men were dogs. She had actually found a true man of God. Even though she felt ashamed of her actions, Ruth was very appreciative of the fact that when she was weak, she could always lean on her partner for strength. This made her love and respect Otis even more.

"You're right, Baby…we shouldn't be doing this," Ruth said, surrendering. Hugging Otis, Ruth gave him a kiss and said thank you.

After that, the two joked around for a while amid the chirping of crickets, before parting company for the night.

After Otis left, Ruth locked the door behind her, turned the alarm on and headed to her bathroom where she freshened up and proceeded to her sons' room to read them their scripture and kiss them goodnight. The scriptures were usually picked arbitrarily, and tonight Ruth opened the Bible to the book of Romans, Chapter 12; the first two verses of which challenged Ruth. After her sons fell asleep, Ruth went down to the kitchen to prepare breakfast and lunch for the boys. She was all torn inside for allowing herself to go as far as she went with Otis that night, and felt sad about it. After preparing the next day's meals, Ruth went up to her bedroom, closed the door behind herself, and wept from the guilt of knowing that she could have jeopardized her relationship by not heeding Naomi's advice and what the Bible said about living a holy life.

She later called Otis before falling asleep to tell him that she loved him. During their conversation, Ruth needed reassurance that she hadn't negatively affected the relationship. She asked Otis whether he loved her.

Otis, not being one to hide his feelings, unequivocally said yes to her and continued to tell her how much he desired to spend the rest of his life with her and her sons.

Just knowing that her love was still alive comforted Ruth and erased her fears.

The following day started off like always. However, with the threat from Duncan looming in the horizon, Ruth drove her sons to school and explained her situation to the principal, handing her a copy of the restraining order she secured over the weekend. Returning home from the boys' school, she decided to straighten up the home and leave early for work, as she was looking forward to her time with Naomi. At about 11:45, Ruth left for GMNH. When she arrived, Naomi was busy perspiring through her physical therapy (PT). After the PT, Ruth took over from the attending nurse, gave Naomi her bath and lunch, and wheeled her outside in her wheelchair to get some sun, and enjoy the view of the city center overlooked by the GMNH grounds. Naomi was very appreciative of this, and couldn't stop thanking Ruth for being there for her. She explained that she never felt quite satisfied with the regular nurse's care.

During this time, Ruth narrated her entire weekend to Naomi, while leaving out all the not-so-complimentary things she did. She explained the situation with Duncan and how upset she and the boys got that Saturday.

"Oh! I am so sorry to hear that you had a difficult visitor, Sweetie. Are you alright? Hmm! There must be a blessing in store for you for the devil to step in this early in your relationship; in trying to mess it up. Well all I can say is try not to put God on the back burner. Always pray and read your Bible…you need God now more than ever. You are not a child so you know that difficult days are sure to come as we live this life. But always have the assurance that God did not bring you this far to leave you. He will not take you through the dark days when you were out there in the world; and then abandon you now that you are trying to live for him. He will give you peace in the midst of the storm. Always pray and read your Bible! Always! Pray and read your Bible! Do not be afraid to call on God…call on him every time you think of him…and you will soon find out that he is the friend that sticketh closer than a brother. In your quiet moments God by his Holy Spirit will be right there. God is awesome. Take faith my dear; you are highly favored...have faith in God."

Ruth told Naomi that she knew she was in love when Otis offered to go to church with them that Sunday.

Cautioning her, Naomi remarked, "<u>Don't base your love on a man agreeing to go to church with you, my dear…contrary to popular belief, the devil goes to church, too, you know.</u>"

This shut Ruth up for a while, but then she continued to explain to her friend how disappointed she was when Otis did not stay a while longer after service on Sunday.

To this, Naomi responded, "Like you respect your personal time, so does he. We can't be too selfish, and think that everything is about us, you know. Watch out for the small stuff, they can ruin a relationship…don't major on the minor, my dear. Besides, did you tell him you would want him to stay before he left home for service that day?"

"No, it never came up," replied Ruth. "But I was expecting that he would want to stay a little while, since we were having so much fun with each other. And besides, we haven't really spent much time together."

"Your expectations are your expectations, Hon. You have to put yourself in the other person's shoes and understand that until you communicate your expectation to someone else, your expectations are still your expectations and no one else's. You say that he loves you…so if he doesn't do something as simple as that, there must be a reason why. Try to understand where he is coming from, and that will eliminate a lot of frustration. You have to communicate your expectations with each other. Some men are homebodies and some are the outdoorsy type…know the one you have, and play to his strengths. If you like the outdoors and he doesn't, then find a medium. If you have a 'Man,' sometimes he will agree to do what you want and sometimes he'll expect you to compromise, too. But you cannot get there if you do not communicate with each other…that is what this courting stage is supposed to accomplish. It's not all about sex, but getting to knowing each other and your tendencies. Some people concentrate on sex and the pleasure it brings, while paying little or no attention to the other 80% of their partner's character and tendencies.

"By the way, when did Otis leave your house last night?" Naomi asked inquisitively.

"About fifteen minutes after we spoke. I had to put the boys to bed," Ruth replied, with a look of innocence that would have made even Mother Mary proud. Ruth also asked Naomi if she knew Otis as someone with a light appetite, because he didn't finish his food that she so carefully prepared.

Naomi smiled and said, "He does eat a lot, and I am sometimes surprised at where the food goes, seeing he doesn't carry a lot of weight to show for it." Sensing that her response didn't sit well with Ruth, Naomi continued, "He must have eaten before you went out for your drive. Did you ask him about it?"

"I sure did, and that was the answer he gave me," Ruth retorted.

"Honey," Naomi began, "contrary to popular belief, the shortest way to a man's heart is not through his stomach. If that were the case, only good cooks would have lasting relationships. Take me, for example, I can't cook to save my life, but my dear Elliot stayed with me all these years. He loved me, Ruth…he really did. But back to your concern. Don't get yourself all worked up over petty stuff, okay? Remember, dear, life's too short for you to spend your time arguing or fussing over trivial things."

# DISCUSSION

1) Was Otis being presumptuous in thinking that Ruth loves him? If not, on what was he basing his confidence?

2) Have you ever been faced with a choice between standing for love and walking away for peace?

3) Why do you think it is difficult to behave chastely even though you do not consider yourself, unequally yoked in your faith? Will you classify a passionate kiss as a chastely behavior?

4) What would have been your advice to Ruth if she was unable to secure Brian and Marcus's approval of Otis?

5) From Naomi's advices thus far, which one is most applicable to your life?

# PART III

# LOVE'S REQUEST

# The Competition

*"What the superior man seeks is in himself. What the mean man seeks is in others."* — *Confucius*

After a good fill of the sun and beautiful weather, the two ladies decided to go back to the room, as it was approaching 2:15, and time for Ruth's shift to start.

As Ruth wheeled her friend along, Naomi turned to her and asked, "How would you like to leave this job and come take care of me at my home instead of coming here, when I am healed a little bit more…just you and me all day long?"

"That would be nice…but on the other hand, I don't want to lose my benefits for my sons. Anyway, let me think about it…I think that would be great," replied Ruth.

"One more question," Naomi continued. "Do you know a nurse by the name of Johnson?"

"Well," began Ruth, as she ran through the names of the nurses at GMNH. "We have about seven on staff whose last name is Johnson… if my memory serves me right…by the way, male or female?"

"Female of course," Naomi retorted.

"Anything else I can go with? Did someone misbehave or do something I should know about?" she inquired.

"No, nothing…just checking…Hmm! Just look at those spider webs up there by the ceiling fan." Naomi pointed as they went down the hallway.

Back on her bed, Naomi beckoned to Ruth to come closer, and then gave her a hug as she thanked her for her help and a beautiful day. It was the first time in a long time that she had seen the sun, birds flying, or even squirrels playing. It was a refreshing and relaxing day for Naomi and she couldn't wait to tell her sons about the wonderful day she had with Ruth. With Naomi healing from her injuries with the help of her physical therapies, she told her sons how much Ruth meant to her, and that she would appreciate it if she could be released to go back home. They didn't want her to stay at home by herself and so she suggested an alternative of staying with Ruth and her sons instead. Unfortunately, Ruth's home was not designed to accommodate her wheelchair, and the flight of steps would make it difficult for her to move around. Saddened by this fact, and wanting to have Ruth all to herself throughout the day instead of sharing her with other patients, Naomi realized that she had become attached to her friend. Larry and Edwin thought about asking Ruth to quit her job with the nursing home and working full-time for their mom. They even thought about asking Ruth to move in with their mom, since her home was a mini-mansion, but knew it would be inappropriate. This was becoming a problem for them, knowing that the one person who could help their mom was Ruth, but unable to figure out how to approach Ruth with this discussion; especially after Naomi had made mention about Ruth's relationship with Otis. Larry and Edwin knew they had to figure out something, and figure it out really fast. They wanted to approach Otis, but didn't want to disrespect him in the process, so they got their thinking wheels turning.

Ruth reported for duty and started her shift with love in her heart. She had spoken to Otis about four times already that day, and she still couldn't wait to hear his voice. She even changed the station that aired in the PA system from classical music to Smooth Jazz, 96.3 F.M. Ruth Moore was in love. During her shift, still curious as to why Naomi had asked her about a Nurse Johnson, she took the time to ask the rest of the staff if they overheard anything about a Nurse Johnson on staff. Except for Stevie, the maintenance clerk who seemed to always know everything about everyone under the sun, no one really heard much, because all the nurses with the last name Johnson worked on either the early or late shift. Stevie was the unofficial gossip coordinator and always had the 411 on all administrative, personnel, and personal issues at the nursing home. He overhead Ruth asking the other nurses as he walked by "minding his business."

Later, when Ruth was alone at her station, Stevie stopped by with his mop bucket and said, "I think I know who you are asking about...you must mean, Brenda...yep...that's who you want," he continued. "She likes rubbing-up on all the big guys...yeah, it's Brenda alright...if anything goes wrong with the last name, it must be Brenda." He continued pushing his mop bucket as he shook his head in disappointment.

Brenda Johnson was a beautiful twenty-eight-year-old nurse who happened to have a little bit more of everything that Ruth considered her endearing qualities...bigger cup size, thinner waist line, firmer thighs, standing 5'10" tall, fairer in complexion, single with no children, an RN with a master's degree, witty, and a snob. In fact, she was the reason Ruth decided to stay with the second shift, since the male administrators had a hard time asking Brenda to work the second shift when she came on board, despite Ruth's seniority and the fact that she had requested a scheduling change shortly before Brenda was hired. Ruth had forgotten about Brenda, and but for her name on the roster, hadn't seen much of her lately; not even when she come in early to be with Naomi. Apparently, Brenda had set her own work schedule. She now skipped her lunch breaks and left an hour early, a privilege that no one else in the establishment was afforded.

Bothered by the fact that her nemesis was around, and with Naomi's cryptic conversation leaving her grasping for straws, a sick feeling came over Ruth. Waiting impatiently for her break period so that she could go ask Naomi to explain herself, Ruth called Stevie over the PA system to her station. As soon as he showed up, Ruth asked him.

"Okay, talk to me. What's going on that I need to know about?"

Smiling with pride that his service had been summoned, Stevie began, "Now, you didn't hear this from me...but I think she's after your man."

"What?" asked Ruth, as if oblivious and puzzled by what Stevie was suggesting.

"C'mon it's me you're talking to...I know...you, Swifty? C'mon now!"

Smiling, Ruth succumbed. "So, what did that heifer do?"

"I don't know," replied Stevie, chuckling as he walked away.

"Hey Stevie, c'mon now, talk to me...lunch is on me tomorrow."

But he just kept on walking, which was his M.O.; leaving snippets, and letting them take root. Feeling her blood pressure rise up in her, a disease she with which she had some struggles since she broke up with Duncan, Ruth was fast becoming the lady she wanted to forget...the one who spoke her mind and then let the chips fall where they may...the one who would stand up and fight if pushed hard enough...the one with a short fuse and unquenchable thirst for revenge. That Ruth was no prissy lady, she was the one who could have made Ares the god of war cry. The feelings came over Ruth again, and her thoughts went into a tailspin as she waited for her break period to start.

*Maybe this was the reason he didn't want to stay after church… who the hell does she think she is? This is what I was warning Naomi about. I can't afford to hurt my boys again…that hussy took my position and now she wants to take my man…the devil is a liar…* Ruth was getting upset, and she knew it was going to be hard to control herself if she continued thinking about Otis or Brenda.

She tried to clear her mind, but this was 'mission impossible,' and she was boiling inside. The more she thought about it, the angrier she got, becoming unbearable as she trembled in anger. Ruth saw herself in a familiar position, the last one standing when the music stopped, and it was tearing her up inside.

Her break period started, but Ruth had lost her appetite. She knew her blood pressure was at a critical level, so she quickly swallowed a couple of pills of her medication and dashed over to Naomi.

As soon as Naomi took sight of her friend, she exclaimed, "Oh Lord! Whatever happened to you? Are you okay? You don't look so good…come sit, you need to see a doctor…your eyes are not right."

"A doctor is actually what I don't need now…tell me, what do you know about Brenda and Otis; and why do men cheat?" Ruth asked as she tried to control her voice and anxiety, to keep from taking her frustration out on Naomi.

"The question is not 'why do men cheat?' Honey. It's 'why do people cheat?' For men, it's probably because they act on their emotions, as cheating or having an affair with multiple partners is viewed by a good number of them as proof of their virility and appeal; while for us, there is a snare attached to cheating, so we usually restrain ourselves and just burn inside when we are attracted to a man other than our partner. It's not just men, Baby...its people. We are prone to yearning for the forbidden fruit...always thinking that the grass is greener on the other side and always wondering, 'What am I missing if I don't?' Anyway, I don't know much about Nurse Johnson, I only overheard some things on the hallway, and she did the rounds with Dr. Swift last Friday...I didn't like her body language...her uniform was too revealing at both ends, and she was not acting like a lady when they came around. I will suggest you talk to Otis and set the record straight, my dear. I am sure it's nothing. Otis is not that kind of man...but <u>one thing you have to remember is that no one's love is worth dying for. Remember, you have two sons to live for. You can't make him love you, God can...so hold on to God."</u>

God! God! God! That name, that name...it always shone the spotlight on Ruth's imperfections as she saw herself through his holiness. Since she decided to turn her life over to God and become a Christian, it had always been Ruth's desire to please him. She has always been faithful, well almost always...when a man was not in her life. Ruth somehow couldn't seem to find that balance or walk the thin line between being a Christian, and being in love. For Ruth, God and her romantic life had been mutually exclusive. Whenever she was "in love," her church attendance dropped, her prayer time somehow diminished, and her holiness dissipated. But this time, Ruth wanted it to work, she needed it to work, and was prepared to do whatever it took as long as she could keep both God and Otis in her life.

Ruth's conscience slowly slid her thoughts back to her previous night's indiscretion. She couldn't ask for forgiveness in front of Naomi as she had acted "the saint," but everything within her told her that she was reaping the fruits of her sin. Ruth knew that even though she didn't cross the line with Otis, her thoughts and actions were just as bad as sinning. She knew that was not becoming of a Christian lady, and was ashamed of herself.

Sobbing uncontrollably under the weight of her guilt and built-up frustration, Ruth whispered, "I can't take this…I have to go home…I am tired…my head is hurting, and I need to lay down." Wiping the tears from her eyes, she told Naomi, who was now also upset on her behalf, "I will see you tomorrow. I have to go home," as she got up and left the room.

Her assistant had stepped out for a break, so Ruth called her on her cell phone, and told her that she had to take the rest of the night off as she was not feeling well. Then she quietly slipped out of the nursing home without anyone seeing her in such a terrible state. Ruth got in her car and drove to her favorite crying spot, the empty parking lot at the church. There she cried her tear banks dry as she apologized to God and pleaded for another chance. She remembered a statement Naomi had made in one of their earlier conversations, "You cannot love anything or anyone else more than you love God."

She knew she was guilty of thinking of Otis more than she did of God or even her sons, lately, and she was sorry.

Still, Ruth was upset with Otis and Brenda and promised herself not to call him or pick up his calls until she felt he was deserving of another chance. *After all, he should have enough sense not to be messing around with that heifer, when he knew he was with someone else.* Ruth protested within.

Feeling a lot better about the fact that God had seen her tears, and how sorry she was, Ruth applied some makeup and drove home to her sons. Pleasantly surprised at Ruth's early arrival, the boys ran to the garage to help her in, only to find that Mom was not feeling well. Marcus carried her purse in as Brian helped her onto the sofa. Worried that she was coming down with something, the boys offered a variety of things from water, to juice, her medication, to even a foot massage, hoping that they would relieve her pain and/or head-ache. Ruth appreciatively turned them down and kindly asked that they secure the house and turn the nightlights on, as she went to bed to rest a while.

"Did you call Dr. Swift to let him know you are not feeling too good? Do you want us to give him a call?" the boys asked.

"No, dear," Ruth replied as she slowly walked up the stairs.

Feeling sad that their favorite lady didn't feel much of herself that evening, Marcus asked if Ruth would mind them reading a pas-sage of scripture to her in turn. Smiling, Ruth declined and reassured the boys that she just needed some rest. Knowing that Otis would probably be trying to reach her later, Ruth turned off her cell phone, took a couple of headache tabs, and settled in to rest.

In the meantime, Naomi had called Otis and scolded him for making Ruth upset. She told him that his indiscretions with Brenda finally made the nursing home gossip headlines and now that precious girl, Ruth, was upset and had to go home. With Otis feeling victimized because he was innocent, he reassured Naomi that Ruth was the last person on earth he would ever dream of hurting. He said he would try to reach out and make it up to Ruth for the embarrassment and shame he might have caused her, even though he hadn't done anything wrong and didn't even realize that Brenda was coming on to him.

"You better!" Naomi exclaimed, and slammed the phone in his ear before he could utter another word.

Otis in all his life had never heard Naomi so upset, and this made him even more worried about Ruth. He tried calling Ruth on her cell, but to no avail. He left messages until her voice mail was full. Still worried about Ruth, and wanting so badly to explain himself, Otis called her house phone and Brian picked up the call. When Otis asked to speak with Ruth, Brian responded that she came home early with a headache and was now asleep, but he would give her the message in the morning. Otis didn't like that, but had to give it up because he had no way of getting past Brian or Marcus without further upsetting Ruth.

Ruth woke up around midnight with a slight headache; still reeling from the gossip about Otis and Brenda. She freshened up and then took a walk over to the boys' room to see how they made out. The boys were fast asleep, so Ruth walked downstairs, made sure the house was secured, and proceeded to prepare the next day's meals for her sons. The aroma of the dishes woke the boys up and they went downstairs to join their mom and see if she was feeling a lot better. Ruth told them she was all right, kissed them on the forehead and asked them to go back to bed. They did so, after Brian had told her that Dr. Swift had called earlier. After finishing downstairs, Ruth turned the lights off and went back to her room, where she said her prayers and updated her wisdom journal, before settling down in bed to check her cell phone messages. It was message central. There were seventeen calls from Otis and one from Naomi. Naomi was worried about her friend and told her that she would be praying for her. Otis's messages, on the other hand, were repetitions of apologies, expressions of love, promises to always be faithful, assurances of commitment, and denials of allegations. His messages were touching and this brought a smile to Ruth's face. She knew Otis was hers. Turning off her cell phone again for fear of letting on her feelings towards him, should they have a conversation, Ruth settled down to sleep, but couldn't, as her mind wandered through her options in ensuring that Otis clearly understood her love should not be taken for granted.

# The Lesson

*"What a vast difference there is between knowing God and loving Him." —Blaise Pascal*

The following morning, Otis called the house phone after the boys were off to school, knowing that Ruth would have to pick up the call as her cell was still off. Even though she had forgiven him, Ruth instinctively hung up the phone as soon as she heard his voice on the other end of the line.

*Wow!* Otis thought. *She must be really angry at me.*

Ruth shook her head in disbelief as she asked herself, *What's wrong with me?*

She couldn't bring herself to call him back, so she went on about her day while silently praying that the Lord would touch Otis's heart to let him call her again. Arriving at work an hour early so that she could talk to Naomi. Ruth crossed paths with Brenda at the elevator as she left work for the day. Brenda greeted her out of innocence, and Ruth gave Brenda a cold stare that would have made Medusa shiver.

She walked over to see Naomi, who out of concern for her friend had managed to work up a fever and was now having one of her worst days at the nursing home. This made Ruth feel guilty, and ashamed to know that her personal life had put a patient's health in jeopardy. As a nursing supervisor, she should have known better, and for this she wasn't proud. At the sight of her friend, Naomi smiled and tried to prop herself up on the bed. Ruth quickly dropped her purse on the chair and proceeded to make her friend comfortable. She apologized for her behavior the previous night and promised not to let her personal life get in the way of her duties.

"Oh shush!" retorted Naomi. "It's not you, it's this place. When you are not around, it's not the same. The staff don't care as much, and they don't take pride in their work…just look at that towel sitting in the sink…it's been there since eight o'clock this morning… the nurse was supposed to take it away after I freshened up, but she just threw it over in the sink and left when her cell phone rang, saying, 'I have to take it…it's my Boo,' whatever that is." Naomi shook her head in disappointment.

"Anyway," she continued, "how are you? I was worried about you. Did you talk to Otis? I called him last night and scolded him… he said he was going to fix it, did he?"

"I guess he tried, but I didn't talk to him…he left a bunch of messages, but I was too upset to hear anything from him," Ruth stated. "He claims that he didn't do anything wrong and that it was just a rumor…in fact, it was Brenda who was flirting with him, but it takes two to tango, and he should not have put himself in that position."

"Trust, Precious, trust. It is the very tenet upon which our society is built. We trust the next man to do his part. Your employer trusts you to conduct yourself professionally and be productive at work, and you trust your employer to compensate you at payday…not written, it's called a psychological contract. We trust our government to provide basic services for us, while the government trusts us to be law-abiding and productive citizens. That's called a social contract. Likewise in a relationship, you and your partner trust that each would be faithful and seek the best of every opportunity presented for each other with respect. That's called, Love. That's all we have…It is way too important to lose over a simple misunderstanding. Tell me the truth, do you trust him and believe what he is saying?" Naomi asked.

Rolling her eyes in defiance, Ruth replied, "Well, yeah I do. But I have to make sure he learns his lesson and never does that again."

"How do you intend to do that, my dear?"

"I could flirt with another man and then let him see how it feels. But since I don't have anyone around here I would dream of flirting with, I would just give him some time apart so that he could think about what he's done."

"Child, please! You said you believe him, right?" Naomi asked. "Don't try to punish him in the process of trying to prove your point over a misunderstanding. It doesn't pay for you to build your happiness on someone else's unhappiness, my dear. You have to be careful how you treat each other, my dear, because 'I am sorry' is sometimes very hard to accept. Especially when it comes to matters of the heart. Forgiveness is a process, Ruth; it is a painful process that is sometimes overlooked when overshadowed by lust. In handling misunderstandings, be objective…think with your head and not your heart or emotions, Darling…don't try to make him jealous in the process. It doesn't work well with some men. Contrary to popular belief, most men are not fighters when it comes to love… if their faith and pride in your love is shaken, they will either walk away from the relationship or mistrust you for a long, long time. It takes a lot of work to regain that trust…you don't want that. I know that payback's a bitch, Sweetie — *pardon my French* — but you're not, so don't cut off your nose to spite your face. You see where I am going with this, Honey?

"Okay, hypothetically, let's say the person you're in love with is unfaithful or abusive to you. Would you disregard your values and become violent or abusive in order to seek vengeance for what he or she did? I wouldn't! I wouldn't minimize my values. Conscience, my dear…"Conscience is a dreadful thing that accuses both mind and body". I have learned. I would rather walk away and make sure I do not put myself in a position where I'd be hurt again. And besides, vengeance belongs to the Lord. As Christians, we have been taught to forgive, but one thing you need to know is that forgiveness has nothing to do with consequences. Don't let anyone walk all over you, either physically or emotionally, to the point where you start feeling like you are unworthy of their presence, and then you decide to stick around because of love. Don't ever make that mistake, my dear…don't you ever do that. That's not what love is all about. Read and study 1 Corinthians, chapter 13 when you get home.

"Respect and trust are two difficult things to get back in a relationship. So when you've got them, don't play games on trivial stuff to prove a point…you will win the battle but end up losing the war. In fact, if you make your partner jealous over you, some would go as far as getting in a fight. The reason for this is not primarily so that they would have you back, but just so the other man can't have you. The object of their passion changes from you to them. Be smart about it, Baby. If you love your partner, don't let him be, in the hope that he would realize your worth and come running. An idle mind is the devil's workshop, you know. He could pick up something you are not prepared to handle when he returns. This goes for both men and women, Ruth, it surely does. Pick up the phone and talk to him…if you don't communicate on something as simple as this misunderstanding, how do you expect to handle the boulders life will throw at you? Oh yeah! Life has some things to throw, alright, and they sometimes come in waves. There will always be someone more beautiful than you…so be happy with who you are, what you have, and be confident in the love you give and share. This fight is not about you, it's about what you're fighting for. So be careful of the decisions you make. Another thing, if you know you tend to have a contentious spirit, that is, as soon as someone mentions 'A,' something starts rising up in you and you feel the need to put up a fight for 'Z,' even though 'Z' was not in the conversation, always make sure you ask God to breathe his 'Peace' into your life. And make sure you have that contentious spirit under control before you start inviting people into your life, be it boyfriend, girlfriend, or even a prayer partner. No one needs to be subject to such an aggravating or contentious spirit."

*Wow!* thought Ruth. *This is tight, but its right...it is so what I need...who is this lady? She is so full of wisdom.* Through Naomi's wisdom, Ruth saw herself and her frailties as expressed by what she thought, said, and did. *If only I had all this wisdom before going through all these trials. This is making too much sense for it to be by accident...I know there must be a reason why both Naomi's and my lives have intersected at this point in time.*

Otis called again, later that day, still trying to plead his case. He wanted to send some roses, but knew he had exhausted his flowery campaign. All he could do was to talk to Ruth and pray that she could see his heart. Picking up the phone, even though her anger had melted away like the wax on Icarus's wings at the sound of Otis's voice, she couldn't help herself but to coldly say, "We need to talk!"

To this, Otis gladly agreed, for it was time he cleared his name. The two agreed to meet the following day for lunch at the park, as Ruth couldn't find a way to eat and still act mad at him. During her break, Ruth told Naomi that she would be meeting Otis the next day so that they would discuss this situation.

Concerned, Naomi asked, "He's not meeting you at home is he?"

"No! I should know better," said Ruth, smiling, as she remembered the times she had tried to discuss issues in the past with her exes, but somehow ended up in makeup sex. "No, not in this relationship," she remarked, with a determined expression on her face.

Ruth met with Otis the following day and he apologized and expressed how sorry he was to have caused such hurt to someone he loved. He explained that Brenda was always flirting with all the men at GMNH, and that he would never give her the time of day, knowing how obnoxious and rude she was to people.

"It's you that I love, Ruth," Otis pleaded. "From the first time I saw you, I couldn't stop thinking of you. Now that I'm getting to know you, Brian and Marcus, I love you even more. I spend my morning yearning for you, my afternoons thinking of you, and my nights wishing for you. I rush to the phone whenever it rings, hoping to hear your voice. It's sad to say but it's true — because of you, I now call on God more often, asking that he'd keep us in love forever. Not an hour goes by that I don't think of and pray for you, Brian, and Marcus. My dreams are nightmares if you are not in them. Every thought of you brings a smile to my face. When I told you I loved you, I meant for always. I never knew what happiness was until I found you...for the first time in my life, I am truly happy,

Ruth. You mean the world to me, and I need you in my life. Ruth Moore, I love you…I truly do. I don't know what my life will be like without you…and I don't intend to find out…I will do anything you ask…just to let you know how much I love and care for you. You have made my life…"

"Oh, stop it, and come here," Ruth interjected, as she grabbed Otis and gave him a hug, kissed him, and whispered, "Don't do this to me again, okay? I love you, but I don't want to be hurt again."

"I promise I will never do anything intentionally to hurt you, Honey. But if we should ever have some kind of misunderstanding, please, please, please, let's talk about it. We have to be able to communicate, if we feel so strongly about each other," Otis pleaded.

This was a wake-up call for Ruth. Having promised God to do right, and wanting so desperately for this relationship to work out for her, she moved cautiously in her interactions with and thoughts of Otis.

During the next four months, Otis became a welcome guest at Ruth's home, attended the boys' baseball and football matches and school activities with Ruth, and took the boys to professional sports games. They spent time together on weekends, sometimes prayed together over the phone, and most importantly ironed out their differences amicably. Meanwhile, Ruth matured as a lady, and with advice from Naomi strengthening their roots in her mind, she handled herself well in situations of conflict that arose in her life, whether with Otis or co-workers.

As Ruth's birthday approached, Otis wondered what would be the ideal and most romantic gift he could give the lady in his life... the one who made him happy without even trying...the one who filled his every thought, and around whom his world revolved. Otis sensed he was almost fulfilled with Ruth, Brian, and Marcus being in his life...he knew he would *be* fulfilled if he could call them his own. He wanted to take the next step, but was unsure of Ruth's response, as she hadn't been passionate with him since that night on her porch after that first Sunday spent together.

Gradually, Ruth was growing more and more in love with Otis and silently wondered about his apprehensions and if he would ever propose to her. She knew he was head over heels in love with her, but couldn't figure out if he was waiting for the traditional timeline of a year before proposing and another year before getting married.

*Or probably he wants to surprise me on my birthday...that would be a great romantic present...it would make my day,* she thought. Her previous proposals were "forgettable." She didn't expect much and didn't get much. *I know Otis is no cheapskate, and whatever he decides to do will be admirable,* Ruth reassured herself.

# Men's Day

*"It takes months to find a customer . . . seconds to lose one. Do not follow where the path may lead. . . go instead where there is no path and leave a trail." —Vince Lombardi*

A couple of weeks before Labor Day, Otis paid Naomi a personal visit and asked her about what gift she thought was best for Ruth on her upcoming birthday. Naomi didn't give him much to work with, but just told him to be creative and make it a day for Ruth to remember. Not quite satisfied with Naomi's response, Otis proceeded to secretly ask Brian and Marcus what they thought their mom would really love and what they would like to give her that would make her really happy. Suggestions from their youthful minds were a diamond necklace, cruise vacation, fur coat, a car, a birthday party, money, a dishwasher, and even a new vacuum cleaner. Otis told both Brian and Marcus to each make their shopping list. The men agreed to keep it a secret, and together they would go out and pick up the presents for Ruth that weekend. Otis asked Ruth for permission to have the boys on Saturday, explaining he needed help with moving some furniture around at his house, and that he'd like to treat the boys to a "men's day out." Ruth volunteered to help out, but was gracefully turned down and told, "It's a man thing." Besides, she could use that time to relax and catch up on some sleep since she had been really busy at work, with a full complement of occupied beds at the nursing home. Knowing something was up and sensing that her men were trying to work on something for her birthday, she allowed the men to spend the day together without her. Trying to pry some information from the boys, Ruth was pleasantly surprised that neither Brian nor Marcus was letting her in on their conversation with Otis. She appreciated the fact that her boys were maturing into men.

That Saturday, Otis picked up Brian and Marcus, who had been anxiously looking forward to this shopping trip, at about 10:30am, and they headed over to a nearby diner for breakfast. The excitement had suppressed the boys' appetites. As they sat to eat, Otis decided they would come up with a game plan by reviewing the lists to eliminate redundancy, and figure out the stores they needed to visit, to minimize their travels. He then gave the boys $1,000 each to spend, which lit up their eyes with a collective, "Whoa!" This was the most amount of money the boys had ever seen or handled, and they were appreciative. Tears choked Otis when he read the joy the boys felt. They were grateful to be able to buy their mom something they figured would make her happy. They had never had someone in their lives who cared for them and their mom the way Otis did, and they were thankful for him. Marcus got up from his seat, went over to Otis, and gave him a hug. Brian did the same. The moment was exciting.

After a cup of orange juice and picking the sausages and ham from their plates, the men headed off to their first stop, the mall. Stopping at an electronic store, Brian picked up an iPad for Ruth and Marcus found a DVD player. Remembering Ruth humming "Hopelessly Devoted" some time back, Otis picked up a couple of CDs for her, including *The Best of Olivia Newton-John*, and *The Best of the Commodores*. That stop lasted twenty minutes; ten of which was attributed to the gift-wrapping. Next stop, Sam's Club. Brian wanted a new vacuum cleaner for his mom, and Marcus remembered seeing the family-size Danish Butter Cookies, and Animal Crackers Ruth sometimes snacked on and took to work. Next stop, Macy's. The boys each wanted to buy Ruth some fragrances, a pair of shoes, and an outfit for church. At Otis's suggestion, they decided to forego the shoes and clothes and pick up the fragrances. Brian got Ruth a bottle of Chanel No.5 perfume, and a gift set of Coco Mademoiselle. Marcus got her a gift set of Anaïs Anaïs and a bottle of Jean Paul Gaultier for women. This was great. They still had some money left, and it was only 12:45pm. Thinking hard and long, Brian asked if they could go back to Sam's. He thought Ruth would really like a flat screen TV, and so they headed back. However, when they got back to the store, reality set in for Brian, as he realized he didn't have enough to cover the cost of the TV after his purchases.

Seeing the disappointment on Brian's face as he looked at a fifty-inch high definition set, which cost $1,800, Otis asked the boys how much they each had left. Together, it was about $650 plus change, and the math didn't add up for the flat screen. Otis then decided to make up the difference they needed to buy the TV, on the condition that they would promise to have all A's on their next report card, to which they agreed. Making A's was a no-brainer for Brian and Marcus, as they were model students who made the President's list at school. He told them that they should continue doing very well in school if they wanted to be in a position where they could provide for their loved ones and even be a blessing to others. Picking up the TV, they decided to take their purchases over to Otis's home before they settled down for lunch. The deal was that Otis would keep their purchases in a room over at his house until Ruth's birthday, when he would bring them over. After moving some furniture around in the visitor's bedroom to make room for the presents, the men each wrote their names on their presents and left for lunch.

After lunch, they stopped over at Wal-Mart, picked up some wrapping paper, bows, tape, and cards for Ruth, went over to a dealership to pick out a car for Ruth, and headed back to Otis's, where they wrapped their presents to the best of their abilities. The day was still young, and so the men decided to settle in the living room, relax, and watch a movie. Tired from the excitement and heavy lunch, it didn't take long for the three to fall asleep as the lonely movie played to the snore-filled room.

Ruth, sensing that her men were out shopping for her, had decided to pay a surprise visit to Naomi, with the intention of taking Naomi out to the back lawn for a picnic. After straightening up around the house that morning, Ruth neatly packed a picnic lunch and put it in a duffle bag together with a CD player and some of her favorite classical CDs to share with Naomi. Figuring the sun could be too much for Naomi, Ruth also decided to take a beach umbrella from her garage with her for shade.

Naomi was glad to see her friend, and not knowing what Ruth had planned for them, the two ladies settled down for a wonderful day together. Ruth brushed Naomi's hair, changed her clothes, grabbed her Bible, some blankets and some pillows, and the two headed out to the back lawn for their time in the sun. They were assisted by a nurse who helped Ruth carry the stack of pillows and blankets. Ruth told Naomi that her men were out and she suspected they were out shopping and planning for her birthday.

Naomi didn't mention that Otis had visited her, but cautioned Ruth, "Hold on to love regardless of the gift. At the same time, don't let him buy his way into your heart. You see, if that's the case, only the rich would be in love. Don't go after what he can give you, Baby. Go after his heart...if you win his heart, he will be incapable of saying, 'No' to you. Just like the Bible says in Matthew 6:33, 'But seek ye first the kingdom of God, and his righteousness; and all these things shall be added unto you.' The things always come after you've got the heart; which in this case is God's righteousness. I know every man has his own price. Some people like jewelry, expensive gifts, and money, while others are into sentimental stuff. Whatever floats your boat, Honey, just don't put your price up on the billboard."

It was a gorgeous day, low seventies, with a mild wind, and the back lawn was nicely mowed. Spreading a thick blanket on the lawn, and nicely padding it with some pillows, Ruth gently assisted her friend on to the blanket and made sure she was comfortable, after which she took out the sandwiches, drinks, a cassette player and a Bible. Naomi was pleasantly surprised...she was having a picnic with her friend. The last picnic she remembered was with her Elliot, and this gave her some mixed feelings. Holding back her tears, she thanked Ruth for her kindness and told her she really appreciated her as a friend. The two ladies had a wonderful day reading their Bibles and enjoying their picnic. Smiling while occasionally bursting out in laughter, taking cat naps, and listening to Classical music accompanied by the gentle breeze. Birds joined in the chorus, and squirrels and chipmunks playfully danced to each overture, as the sun played hide-and-seek from behind the fluffy clouds; Naomi was at peace and later admitted: "This is very nice. Who knew living in a nursing home would be this pleasant? Actually it wouldn't, if not for your warmth and love."

Watching from their windows, some of the other nursing home residents grew a little jealous of Naomi and inquired how come they couldn't go out in the sun as the other patient. The response they got back was if they could find someone to take them out and sit with them without putting their health in danger, and with approval from their physicians, they were also free to go lay out in the sun, too. Unfortunately, most nursing home residents didn't have loved ones who would give of their time to accommodate them in this manner.

After five hours out in the sun, they decided to call it a day and return to the room. Ruth called the nurse who assisted them, and with her help, they were able to return Ruth's stuff back to her car. The blankets and pillows were taken to the laundry room by the nurse, who had changed Naomi's beddings while the two ladies were having their picnic. It was a great day. Ruth called Otis and asked if they were having a great day and he sounded excited and told her that their day couldn't have been any nicer.

Early that evening, Otis drove the boys back home where Ruth was waiting expectantly to see if they would be carrying any gift bags with them. She was disappointed but happy to see the smiles on their faces, knowing that her sons had spent a wonderful day with the man she loved. She asked them about their day and all she got back was that after moving the furniture around, they had a heavy lunch and watched a movie. After preparing and serving a light dinner, Ruth spent the evening with her men, watching a made-for-TV movie on ABC Family Channel. Since Sunday meant church day, the boys said goodnight to Otis and went upstairs to prepare for service the next day. With Ruth lying across the sofa with her head on his lap, Otis leaned forward and kissed her gently on the lips. Turning her head towards him, Ruth reached for Otis and kissed him passionately.

She was in love with Otis and would have given it all up, but she remembered the promise she made to God and so had to stop and whisper to him, "Let's wait and make it blessed."

Reluctantly, he gently stopped, closed his eyes, and smiled, while thanking his lucky stars that Ruth's love still remained, as he throbbed regressively to a calm. After about fifteen minutes of gently caressing each other, Otis kissed Ruth goodnight and left for his home, still battling with himself over whether it would be appropriate to propose to her.

# Attitude Check

*"I know God will not give me anything I can't handle. I just wish He wouldn't trust me so much."* — *Mother Teresa*

The week didn't go by fast enough. Ruth anticipated Otis's proposal. Brian and Marcus were eager to present their gifts to their mom. And Otis expectantly waited to see Ruth's response when he presented his gift. On top of everything Otis had bought for Ruth when he was with the boys, he had also gone out and spent another $15,000 on a gift he hoped she would appreciate. It was a well thought out and emotional gift, and he had poured his heart into it. Over the years, Ruth had usually worked on Labor Day, as it meant getting paid for time-and-a-half. However, this year she had a new outlook and would rather spend the day with the men in her life. She had scheduled the Monday and Tuesday off from work and was excited about life.

That weekend was great. Ruth spent some time with Naomi on Saturday, barbequed with her men, and played in the rain that Sunday afternoon when the four of them got drenched while taking

a stroll on the boardwalk. It was fun. After arriving home that evening, they dried themselves up, changed their clothes and went over
to Otis's place.

Otis had promised to treat Ruth and her sons to one of his signa-
ture meals a week earlier, and wasn't going to let a little rain spoil
his party. Ruth still had no idea what she would be receiving for
her birthday, as the men had cunningly outwitted her by secretly
hiding the presents under her bed while she was over at Naomi's
that Saturday. This was the last place she ever thought of looking,
and was hoping to find the presents over at Otis's when they went
for dinner. Late that night, with everyone tired, Otis asked them to
spend the night, as he had a four-bedroom house. Cautious, Ruth
graciously turned him down, saying that they didn't come prepared
for a sleepover. It was a beautiful home that Ruth had visited many
times before, but she had never spent the night. Though the invitation was tempting, she wasn't about to start now, at least not with her
sons present. Sometime around 10pm, Otis drove them back home.
When they arrived, Ruth softly asked him to spend the night with
her on the sofa. She felt bad that he had to do all the driving, even
though he was just as tired as they were. He reciprocated and told
her that he didn't leave home with the intention of sleeping over, so
he'd rather drive back to his place. Ruth felt hurt that he would turn
her down, and thought Otis was being spiteful and mean to her.

*How could he?* she thought. *Why is he being so mean to me,
now that I am in love with him?* She thought about her birthday and

how special this day would be, sharing this time with her two sons, and the love she couldn't keep off her mind. Ruth didn't do too well with rejections, and Otis turning her down didn't sit too well with her. She didn't appreciate the fact that he didn't even take the time to think about her offer before saying, no.

She felt betrayed by her emotions, which slowly ushered tears to her eyes. But even though she was hurt, Ruth still waited by the phone in her bedroom, just to hear Otis's voice on the other end of the line as she stared into the darkness of the night.

After he had pulled away and headed home, Otis knew he had hurt Ruth, and became worried that his love would be unhappy. He tried to call her on his cell, but fumbled the phone onto the floor on the front passenger side of his car. As soon as he arrived home, Otis gave Ruth a call to let her know he made it in safe. To his surprise, she sounded as if everything was fine.

Confused, he asked Ruth if everything was all right, to which she replied, "Yes I am. Why shouldn't I be?"

"Well," said Otis, "I thought you were upset because I didn't stay over."

"No, Otis," she exclaimed. "I am not upset because you didn't want to stay over…I am upset because you were being spiteful and mean to me."

"I was not," Otis replied in an octave higher, and continued. "I did not stay over because I respect your decision as a mother not to set a bad example for the boys. I was tired but would rather drive home and put myself in harm's way than to disrespect you, and you can't even appreciate that? It's not all about you, Ruth. Try to think of someone else sometimes."

These words hit home and crushed the walls that Ruth had built since her childhood. She was jarred by reality, as it was the first time Otis had stood up to her.

Softly and in tears, Ruth conceded, "I'm sorry." She knew she was wrong. She was disappointed with herself, and at the same time fell deeper in love with Otis. "I am sorry, please forgive me," she pleaded again.

To which Otis replied: "I am sorry too, baby…you must know that I'd never intentionally hurt you…that's not me…I wish I would have found a more gracious way to explain why I can't stay, when I was over at your place. I was hurt, too, when you said you and the boys couldn't spend the night…I felt you didn't trust me…but then I tried to put myself in your shoes, and knew where you are coming from. Do this for me, too. Believe me…I love you, Ruth, and I can't be mean to you. No, not the way I feel about you."

The two reaffirmed their love to each other for the next hour and a half until Otis, weary from a long day's work fell half asleep on the phone and had to ask Ruth, who was also getting tired, if they could continue their lovely conversation the next day.

Ruth finally knew she was ready for marriage after she realized how unselfish her action was when confronted with a situation that would have tripped her up in the past. Mason, a longtime friend with whom Ruth once had a tryst, was having a party in celebration of his recent promotion to regional president in one of the fastest-growing companies in North America. She was sent a special invitation to attend. Mason gave her an all-expense-paid offer that was hard to refuse, as the invitation came with a business class airline ticket, limousine travel during her stay in Chicago, and a five star hotel accommodation. Ever since their fling, even though the relationship was nothing to write home about, the two had kept in touch over the years and would call each other if anything noteworthy was on the calendar. It would have been easy for Ruth to jump on the next flight out before she met Otis, but now it was different and the battle lines in her mind had already been established.

*I could go if I want to. After all, there is no ring on my finger. Should I tell Otis of this invitation and then leave the decision of whether I should or shouldn't go up to him? I could still inform him about the invitation and then still go. After all, this life is too short for me to let such an opportunity go to waste. Should I just decline the invitation and inform Mason that I am now in a serious relation-ship? Should I still go, and if he wants to try something naughty with me, then inform Mason that I am now in a serious relationship? Should I tell Otis about this invitation and then get some brownie points from him for not going? It's not like I am dating Mason or anything like that. He is just a friend and my conscience is clear.*

After going over each possible solution a few more times than she would have liked, Ruth finally decided to gracefully decline Mason's invitation, without even mentioning the invitation to Otis. Her rationale was that the relationship with Otis was more important to her than the one with Mason, which she considered a non-issue and therefore wouldn't bring it up. Besides, she wouldn't have wanted Otis to be slippery with her if the shoe was on the other foot. Ruth's new philosophy in life of treating people the way she would like to be treated even caught her by surprise, and this epiphany made her a little proud of the maturity and growth into which she was being transformed.

# Ruth's Birthday

*"Life is so constructed that an event does not, cannot, will not, match
the expectation."* — *Charlotte Bronte*

R uth woke up to the smell of fresh coffee, and a "Happy Birthday" duet from Brian and Marcus. The boys had taken the time to prepare breakfast for their mother, who was so grateful that a few tears rolled through. They both gave her a kiss and a hug with their greeting cards and a bottle each of the fragrance they bought. It was arranged between Otis and the boys that they would each give her a perfume and then save the rest of the gifts for later that morning, when Otis came over. Surprised by her sons, Ruth excused herself for a brief while, went to the bathroom to freshen up, and then returned to her treat. She was happy that she could finally get to spend her birthday with her sons. Settling herself in an upright position in the middle of the bed, with her two sons on each side of her, Ruth proceeded to open the birthday cards and then the presents. She'd always tried to teach the boys to save the best for last. This time, however, it was a tall order. Marcus' card read:

*To my Darling Mom…*

*I just want to let you know*

*That wherever I go*

*Be it in land or sky or sea*

*Or even throughout eternity*

*You are the one, the only one*

*Best Mother in the World*

*Happy Birthday!*

*Love, Marcus.*

With tear-filled eyes, she turned to Marcus, who gave her a hug and said. "Happy Birthday, Mom."

Brian's card had a beautiful red rose on a green flowerbed on the cover, and it read:

*"Hi, Mom,*

*I'd like to take this time to say*

*Thank you for all my everyday*

*For your kindness and your love*

*For your unselfishness through it all*

*For your care and your tears*

*And being there through the years*

*For your smiles instead of frowns*

*And standing strong when chips were down*

*May this day and all to come*
*Bring you love and peace and joy.*

*Happy Birthday Mom!*
*Love Always, Brian.*

Now it was official, her tear ducts lost their lids as she hugged her sons and kissed them, whispering, "I love you so much. Thank you…thank you…you have made my day…thank you."

"We love you too, Mom," the boys reassured her, and urged her to open the gifts.

She opened the Chanel No. 5 and was excited, as she had always wanted a bottle, but never had the mind to treat herself. "Thanks, Brian, but where did you get the money to buy this perfume?"

"Don't worry, Mom, your men came together," was his response with a smile.

Turning to Marcus's gift, she was surprised to see a bottle of Jean Paul Gaultier for Women. "Did you pick this out yourself?"

"Yep," Marcus replied.

"You guys have incredible taste…impressive, so let me guess, my men came together, huh?" With a smile, she gave the boys a hug again and said thank you. As the three of them sat on the bed, Ruth asked her sons: "Is this what you guys were doing the other weekend?" while tickling them into bursts of laughter.

After her breakfast in bed, Ruth took her shower, did her hair, and changed into a white blouse, blue jeans, and white sneakers. She applied a slight touch of each perfume on each side of her body and felt like royalty. She got the boys to guess which perfume was on which side, and they were on the money. Shortly after her "guess that fragrance" game, Otis pulled up with nothing but a birthday card in his hand. After last night, she was so much in love with this man that her heart melted at his voice. She gave him a hug and a wet kiss on the lips, in front of the boys, and he blushed and wished her a happy birthday. He handed Ruth the card and as she opened it, she thought, *Please don't tell me this man gave me a gift certificate.* Surprised, she found there was nothing in the card but a simple:

*To the One I Adore…*

*Ruth,*

*Happy Birthday!*

*Forever Love, Otis*


Saying thank you in the most appreciative tone, without seeing even a dollar bill in the card, Ruth thought, *Okay what is he up to now?* She gave him another hug and whispered, "Thank you for the boys."

As per arrangement with the boys, Otis walked Ruth outside on the porch and closed the door behind them, as if wanting to get some more of her juicy kisses. While he hugged her and kissed her playfully on the lips, Brian and Marcus sneaked into Ruth's bedroom and transported the remaining gifts downstairs to the living room.

After about ten minutes of hugs and kisses, Ruth gently put her finger on Otis's lips and asked, "Okay, what do you want?"

Smiling, he replied, "I want you," and then walked Ruth back into the living room, where the boys were waiting, and shouted, "Surprise!"

Surprised, Ruth saw these gifts and knew that this birthday, unlike any other, would be filled with love, joy, and happiness. Marcus then ushered Ruth to a seat on the sofa, where her men took turns presenting their gifts. She knew her sons couldn't afford all these gifts and that Otis had supported them, just so that the boys could share the joy of being able to give of their heart's desires to their mother. Ruth was overwhelmed by all the gifts, as she didn't expect Otis to go to this length in celebrating her birthday. She appreciated all the gifts…her iPad, DVD player, vacuum cleaner, butter cookies and animal crackers, her Coco Mademoiselle and Anaïs Anaïs gift sets, her flat screen TV set, and her CDs from Otis.

This was really neat, and turning to Otis, she smiled and said, "You are unbelievable. Thank you." She gave the boys a hug and thanked her men for making her day so special.

With the laughter in her eyes and love in the air, Ruth still had this nagging voice in her head. She was torn between being happy for what she had received, and not getting a proposal and an engagement ring from Otis. *After all,* she thought, *time is not on my side… maybe he's afraid of commitment, especially after his bitter divorce.*

However, Ruth remembered Naomi's words of wisdom that she should, "hold on to love regardless of the gift." This was a little difficult for her, seeing that the next major holiday was Thanksgiving. Again, time was not on her side; for she dreaded this day, because she turned 40. Masking her internal struggles well, Ruth called Otis to sit beside her as the boys hooked up the new TV and DVD in the living room, replaced the one that was in Ruth's bedroom with the TV from downstairs, and transferred Ruth's set over to their room; and also did a test run of the vacuum. Brian and Marcus surprised Otis and Ruth by knowing a lot more about electronics installation and connection than they thought. A great contentment came over Ruth, seeing the look of joy and accomplishment in Brian's and Marcus's eyes as they rambled on and on about the different features on the flat screen, iPad, and DVD.

At about 1pm, Ruth felt she had to treat her men to lunch, but they insisted that it was her day and that she should relax and be pampered. She agreed to the idea of being treated like a queen on her birthday. Otis drove them to a nearby restaurant that was open for business, where they had lunch. During lunch, seeing his mother all in smiles, Marcus reached over to Ruth and whispered, "Keep smiling, the fun has just begun." This piqued Ruth's curiosity and gave her a clue that all hope was not lost. Maybe, just maybe, Otis would still propose.

After lunch, Otis drove them to his home, using the excuse that he forgot to take his multivitamins earlier that day. Arriving at his place, he asked them in for a while, using the front door to bring them inside, rather than opening the garage door. He invited them into the dining room. Running upstairs to his medicine cabinet, Otis took his meds and hurried down to the dining room to join his guests. He then asked Brian and Marcus to accompany him to the kitchen, where they brought back from the refrigerator a double-decker, chocolate, vanilla, and strawberry birthday cake, with *"Happy Birthday, Ruth…Love O, B, & M!"* written on it.

"Thanks, guys! Wow! Y'all sure know how to make a lady feel special!" exclaimed Ruth.

Otis then inserted a single candle in the middle of the cake and lit the candle as the boys gleefully asked their mom to make a wish. Ruth blew out the candle and made a wish that she refused to share, despite numerous pleas from Brian and Marcus. After cutting the cake in love, and when everyone had a piece, Ruth wanted to take some over to Naomi and her co-workers at the nursing home. Cutting a sizable portion for the staff, and wrapping a piece for Naomi, Otis asked them to use the garage on their way out, since he wanted to lock the front door from the inside.

When they got to the door leading to the garage, Brian volunteered to take the cake from Ruth. As Otis turned to open the garage door, he said: "Happy Birthday, Ruth…I love you." And there as the curtain rose to the brightness of day, exposed in the garage, was a brand new, navy-blue, Mercedes Benz G55 AMG SUV.

Stunned into silence, with eyes wide open, Ruth froze in her path in disbelief. Softly, she asked: "Baby...Why...Is this for me? Oh Lord..." was the last thing she remembered saying, before waking up on the living room sofa at Otis's home. She had passed out in the garage.

"Are you okay?"

"Mom, are you alright?"

"Do you need water?"

Those were some of the questions that greeted Ruth as she regained consciousness a couple of minutes later, to the sight of her men gently smiling at her side.

Slowly collecting herself, she squinted her eyes, looked teasingly at them and remarked, "I'm gonna get y'all for this."

Shaking her head at them in disbelief, Ruth looked across the room in a daze as she reflected on her past...and how no "love" had ever done this much for her, and those who even dared to treat her to dinner had always wanted something back from her, usually sex. Shaking her head as if to wipe away the cobwebs, and coming back to reality, Ruth asked Brian to serve her a glass of water, which she sipped.

Then, determined to enjoy her present, she put out both hands for support as she gingerly rose to her feet and said, "Okay let's go see my ride."

Brian and Marcus were already pleading for her to start driving them to school in the morning. She agreed, knowing that would make them the envy of their fellow students.

Excited, the boys led the way back into the garage, where she surveyed the car, admiring every inch of its beauty. Tinted windows, custom grey leather interior with **Ruth** inscribed on the headrests, and a host of gizmos that would take some getting used to…yes, it was her car…her first brand new car…her first Mercedes Benz…she never lived a life of luxury or accustomed to the finer things in life… yet this was her car…and it was a birthday present from the man she loved, who adored and loved her back. Taking the cake from the dining room table, Otis secured his home and asked Ruth to take the wheel, and they drove over to the nursing home. The drive over to Naomi was a little shaky, as Ruth tried to navigate the road amidst advice from her sons as to which buttons to push and turn.

Arriving safely at the GMNH, Otis asked Ruth if she wanted him to accompany them. At this point, she wanted the whole world to know that she and Dr. Swift were in love with each other. The four of them went up to Naomi, after stopping at the desk to give Ruth's staff their portion of her birthday cake. Naomi was pleasantly surprised. She didn't expect Otis to accompany Ruth and her sons in paying her a timely visit, as she was feeling sad without her family and friend. Naomi sat up on the bed, thankful for the visit, enjoyed the cake, and wished Ruth a happy birthday. Being considerate, she asked Ruth to go and have a great time with her men, and said that they would see each other when she returned to work. It was a forty-five minute visit that brightened her day. She appreciated Otis, Ruth, and her sons for thinking of her.

Ruth's birthday was filled with love, joy, and happiness and she couldn't have asked for anything better. Even though she didn't get her proposal, she felt the love and presents somehow made up for the ring. After leaving GMNH, they took the interstate highway with Ruth still at the wheel; and drove twenty minutes away before turning back, after she asked with a smile not to put too many miles on her new baby. They then drove back to Otis's, where he picked up his car and followed them over to Ruth's. They spent the rest of the evening watching a couple of movies on the flat screen. It was like night and day, compared to their old set. The high definition pictures were so vivid, and the surround sound also brought art to life. Otis wanted to take them out for dinner at a trendy restaurant, but Ruth gracefully declined and asked if they could have leftovers from the barbeque on Saturday instead. Otis appreciated that, even though he had called ahead for a special table, which he now had to cancel.

# The Proposal

*"We all live with the objective of being happy; our lives are all different and yet the same."* — Anne Frank

After dinner, in between movies, Otis got up from his seat and went over to his jacket, which was lying on one of the chairs. Smiling, he walked over to Ruth, and to the surprise of Brian, Marcus, and Ruth, went down on his knees. Looking into her eyes, he opened his hand to reveal a little red box. With a charming smile and love-filled voice, he said: *"Ruth, I know this is your birthday, and I don't want to take anything away from this celebration. I have loved you since the first time I saw you, and every moment in love with you has made me a better man. I find pleasure in hearing your voice, joy in your laughter, and peace when you are around. I've been waiting for this moment to tell you how much I love you, and I can't wait another day to show you how much I care. I know only God can satisfy our every need, and I've asked this much of him, that he will meet my need and keep us together, forever. You are beautiful, Ruth and very attractive. Most of all, you are a lady and a great mother. I know you could choose from any list of men with whom you would spend the rest of your life, but on my knees I beg you this day, let it be me. Ruth Moore, will you marry me?"*

There was a deafening silence in the room, as the boys had muted the sound on the TV and turned their attention to Otis's proposal. Stunned into silence, Ruth could hear the waning echoes of the fears of her past as she stared into the beautiful and brilliant marquis cut diamond and white gold ring. Taking the ring from the box, Ruth put the ring on her finger. It was a perfect fit.

Gently nodding, she stammered, "Yes...I...Will...I will!" Tears streamed down her face at the thought of finally having a man her sons could look up to, one they would someday call dad, who would respect, love, and treat her right. Someone who would be by her side during what used to be her lonely nights.

Hugging him tight, she felt vindicated for being patient and heeding Naomi's words of wisdom, and most of all, for all those years she had no one to call her own. Ruth wiped her eyes and excused herself to the powder room, where she freshened up and admired her ring in the mirror a little bit more before coming out and landing a deep and passionate kiss on Otis's lips.

To see the look in her eyes, the smiles, and the feel of love in the air was worth the moment, Otis thought. All he ever wanted to do since he first laid eyes on Ruth was to love and care for her. He wanted so badly to please her, and most of all, have her to be his wife. Ruth was so unlike his ex-wife, who was never satisfied, inconsiderate, unappreciative, and could have passed for Maris Crane's sister.

Ruth would have given it all to him that night, but she remembered Naomi's words of wisdom: "Don't let him buy his way into your heart." This was a struggle for Ruth, since she felt guilty after receiving all of these gifts and so much love, without giving anything back in return. In trying to find a gift worthy of such outpouring of love, Ruth's mind raced from tangible things to having sex with Otis.

*After all,* she thought, *we are now engaged...I'm sure that God wouldn't consider it a sin.* However, as she struggled between the when and why, she knew deep down inside that it was not the right time, and doing so would just jeopardize their relationship...especially after the trial she had to endure with that hussy, Brenda. She couldn't stand to risk this one, no matter how hot her passion burned.

With the boys still on vacation and Ruth also off from work, Otis stayed over a little later than usual. After watching the second movie, Ruth sent Brian and Marcus, who were exhausted from the day's activities, to bed, so that she could spend some quality time with her fiancé. Staring into each other's eyes and burning in love, Ruth gently smiled and in an apologetic tone with tear-filled eyes, she stated:

"Honey, thank you. I wish I could find the words to say how much I appreciate you. You've done more for me than I could have ever imagined. This is the best birthday ever. The way you made

Brian and Marcus happy, just to be able to give me their hearts' desires…just to see the smiles on their faces. Thank you. I appreciate you."

"Oh, you are most welcome, Babe…you deserve it all and more," Otis replied.

Unable to contain her gratitude, with tears flowing down her checks onto her blouse, Ruth stammered: "It's…it's not so much the gift as it is the happiness you've given these boys. You don't know this, but for their young lives they have experienced a lot of disappointments and just to see the laughter in their eyes and knowing the joy and pride they felt in trying to make me happy…thank you. I truly appreciate you…you don't know how much this means to me…you…"

"Baby, don't cry," Otis interrupted. "I love you and everything is going to be alright. You and the boys can always count on me to be there for you. When I first told you that I love you, it was from the bottom of my heart. I will always love you and I will do anything for you." Hugging each other with the deepest of feelings, they felt the closest to each other than they've ever felt before.

With eyes closed and head resting on Otis's shoulder, Ruth whispered: "I love you so much." And sighed with the satisfaction of knowing that it was her time to love and be loved. Excusing herself to go freshen up, Ruth returned with a burden on her mind.

*Clearly, this man loves me and my sons; he'll honestly do anything for me; he's been nothing short of a gentleman and he respects me and treats me like a lady; since we started dating, he's been the one spending and I am yet to even reciprocate; and now I am feeling like I owe him something. I don't want to be indebted to him, but I have all these things plus the love he shares and yet he has nothing from me to show for our time together. I cannot go out and shop for him because he seems to have everything he needs and more; this isn't right...I cannot go on feeling like I owe my life or happiness to him. All I can give him for now is my love, and maybe my body. Hmm! This wouldn't work...I can't give him my body although I wouldn't mind. No! What we have is too special for me to give it up for a moment's pleasure. I don't know...this is hard. I am sure there's no rule that says you can't have sex when you are engaged...after all, he loves me, I love him, and we are committed to each other... that should be okay, right? I don't know and I'd rather not chance it...better safe than sorry.*

While wrestling with her thoughts, Otis noticed that Ruth had a worrying look on her face and she seemed distant from the heartfelt moment they just shared and so he asked: "Baby, are you alright? Is something bothering you?"

Moving a bit closer to Otis, Ruth hugged him and in the softest of tone acknowledged: "Honey, you know I love you and what we have is very special. I want you and I want to give you all I've got, but I'm scared. Even though I need you...I mean, now...I am afraid of getting God upset at us...I want God to bless this relationship and our marriage...you know?"

Nodding Otis replied: "Baby, I want you too, but let's try to wait. It won't be long we will soon be married…okay?" Though not the response Ruth would have honestly wanted to hear at this moment in time, she was grateful it was what she got.

Understanding the balance upon which this sensitive moment was weighed and to change the subject, Otis asked, "So tell me, when would you suggest?"

This brought a smile back to Ruth's face as she admired her ring, with fingers spread out and eyes sparkling from the glitter of the diamond. "You've got great taste…wow…you're amazing," she complimented Otis. "Baby," she continued, "I know you have spent a lot already on me and I don't want to put any more on you…let's think about it tonight and discuss it tomorrow…is that alright? I wouldn't mind something small, Honey…let's promise not to spend a lot on the wedding, please?"

As a little girl, Ruth had dreamt of a wearing a white wedding gown, getting married in a church, seeing white doves released into the air as she and her husband drove away in their limousine…but all she got were two shotgun weddings at the local municipality building. However, she kept her desire to herself. Seeing everything Otis had done for her and his willingness to please her, she wouldn't dream of putting more burden on him, so she held her peace. They talked for hours regarding the wedding, the wedding party, the guest list, Brian's and Marcus' role in the ceremony…until they both fell asleep in each others' arms on the sofa.

Waking up at about 3am in Otis's arms, Ruth could have pinched herself, but it was no dream. This one was for real. She was lying next to a man who loved and cared for her. She wanted to invite him up to her bedroom, but having been scared straight by Brenda, she wouldn't dare make that suggestion. And besides, she wouldn't want the boys to find them in bed together. Seeing both her and Otis kissing passionately for the first time was enough shock for her sons to endure in one day, she thought.

Otis left at about 5:30am and went back home, where he rolled into his bed and slept like an exhausted baby until a little past midday.

Ruth, on the other hand, didn't bother to make it to her bedroom, but lay back down on the sofa. She held the cushion that captured the lingering fragrance of Otis's cologne close to her breast, as she slumbered in love. Brian and Marcus came downstairs around 10am to find their mother snoring in the living room, fast asleep. They grabbed a bottle of juice, some cookies, and headed back to their room, where they relaxed until Ruth woke up sometime in the early afternoon. After taking her shower, Ruth gave Otis a call, drove the boys over to his place, and then took her men out for lunch. It was her treat, for all the love they showed her on her birthday.

*What a difference a car makes,* Ruth thought, as she was envied and admired by both men and women. The attention she got on the road and when she pulled up at the restaurant was amazing, and she loved it. Later that day, while they were over at Otis's, he handed her a set of keys to his home, an extra garage door opener, and proceeded to give her the password to his security system. It was official: Ms. Ruth was the lady of the house. She looked the part, and loved every minute of it. Time went by quickly, and around 8pm that evening, Ruth kissed her fiancé goodnight, told him she'd call when they had settled down, and then took the boys home to get ready for school and the start of a new semester the next day.

At home, she made sure that her sons were all set for school and tucked up in bed for a restful night of sleep. Then Ruth went into her bedroom, said her prayers, and curled up in bed with the phone to dial the love of her life. They spent a couple of hours on the phone, saying sweet nothings, and then agreed to meet for dinner the next day before playing kissing tag and calling it a night.

Brian and Marcus were up early the next day, ready for another semester, but most of all they were ready for their ride to school. Ruth was already up, knowing how important this day was to Brian and Marcus. She prepared breakfast and lunch for them, then took her shower, got dressed, did her hair and applied some makeup to look like a success in her new Mercedes. After breakfast and saying their prayers, Ruth sat both boys down in the living room and gave them a short word of encouragement to let them know how proud she was of them, and to mentally prepare them to succeed in school that semester. It had always worked, and this time was no different. The only other motivation they needed now was that they also had to make Otis proud of them. They were determined to do that since they had promised him to get all A's while shopping for their mom's birthday presents. After their brief moment of reassurance of love and encouragement, Ruth and her sons headed off to school with Marcus riding shotgun and Brian looking stately, being chauffeured by a beautiful lady he called Mom.

From the time they exited their driveway until pulling up in front of the school, they turned heads, glances into stares, and frowns into smiles. Even the grumpy old crossing guard, Mr. McKinney, allowed them to ride by and stopped the car behind them for a bunch of kids who were sluggishly approaching the cross walk. During their ride to school, Marcus asked his mom a couple of questions that she was not sure of how to respond.

"So Mom, when you and Doc get married, what should we call him, and would you change our names?"

Swallowing the lump in her throat, Ruth thought about it for a few seconds and then tried her version of reverse psychology on her sons.

"What do you think? Okay, let's do this. I want you two to think about it today and we'll discuss it this evening, cool?"

"Yeah, Mom, this evening," the boys agreed, while Ruth's inner voice murmured, *Some things just won't go away,* as she drove her sons to school.

Pulling up in front of the school, all eyes were fixed on the SUV, wondering who in the world was living in such luxury, because the tinted windows made it difficult to see the occupants. Brian reached over the seat and gave his mom a peck on the cheek, followed by Marcus, and the two boys stepped out as if in a choreographed move, shut the doors, gave their mother a thumbs up, then turned and walked into the sea of students as the new pack leaders. Beaming with pride, Ruth slowly pulled away and headed back home.

Ruth hadn't spoken to Naomi since she last visited on her birthday; and so she left for work around midday in order to get in some catching up time. She drove her Ford Explorer and left the Mercedes Benz at home parked in the garage, as she loved her new 'baby' and was very protective of her. Arriving at work, Ruth headed straight for Naomi's room and before she could say, "Hello," Naomi sang out triumphantly, "What's that on your finger? Come here, girl...whoa!...see, I told you, he's the one, have you set a date yet? I have to be there, so make it soon."

The two ladies hugged and laughed in joy. Naomi could see how proud Ruth was and she was happy for her. She knew she deserved it and felt a sense of satisfaction, knowing that she had brought them together.

"So tell, how did it all happen, how was your weekend, your birthday, and everything...just tell me...pull up a chair...I hope you are not clocking in any time soon...'cause I want to hear it all." Naomi chuckled.

"This was the best birthday I've ever had," Ruth began. "Let's see," she recounted. "A bunch of presents from <u>my</u> sons and Otis, a wonderful lunch, a double-decker cake, a brand new SUV, and an eye-popping engagement ring, all mixed in a gravy called love…I couldn't have asked for anything better…you should see the car, Naomi, he took my breath away this weekend…I mean literally."

Smiling at her friend's cheerfulness and good fortune, Naomi pulled Ruth closer and said, "Ruth, honey, Otis is in love with you, he adores you…um ... but you didn't…did you?"

Shaking her head, Ruth was proud to say 'no' with confidence.

"Good for you," continue Naomi. "Anyway, don't mean to burst your bubble, dear, but just a word of caution: be careful how you use the word, 'my' going forward…even if you own the house, and make more money than he does, other than personal effects such as your underwear, watch how you use that word…it's just two letters but it has the power to show possession and also exclusion…so be careful, dear, it could silently have a negative effect on what you have labored to build. Okay, go on."

"Well, I feel somehow guilty for receiving all that stuff and not giving him anything back…you know what I mean…so how can I make it up to him?" Ruth asked.

"Simple," said Naomi. "Your sexuality is your main place of empowerment; so don't give it up for a moment's pleasure…don't make the bedroom dictate your world. Just keep him in close proximity, reaffirm your love for him every chance you get by telling him how much you love, care for and appreciate him. If he really loves you, he will wait for you…and just hurry and set the wedding

<u>date already</u>, for crying out loud…I am not getting any younger you know," she finished, and the two women laughed in joy.

The two ladies went on and on, going over every detail of that weekend and Ruth's birthday. They had a great time together. By the time Ruth reported for duty, word of her engagement had spread all around the nursing home, from two nurses who had stopped by Naomi's room during her visit. There was a buzz in the air and it was a very exciting evening for Ruth, as patients, staff, and even some visitors took the time out to admire her ring. It was official. Word had spread all around that Ruth and Dr. Swift were engaged to be married, and she felt like the queen of the castle.

During her short break later that day, Ruth stopped over at Naomi's room, and was surprised to find a gentleman whom she introduced as her accountant. Agreeing to see Naomi during her second short break, as she had to step out during her lunch break, Ruth left and headed outside to the main entrance, where she stood far from all distractions and called Otis…just to let him know how much she was missing him and looking forward to a hug at dinner.

Ruth was nowhere to be found at the nursing home during her lunch break. She left fifteen minutes early and headed over to the restaurant, where she and Otis were scheduled to have dinner. She was on time, as was he, and the two settled down next to each other, holding hands, and feeding each other as they prayed that time would stand still. The sight of them told all onlookers that love was in the air.

# DISCUSSION

1) Was Ruth justified in her treatment of Otis; relative to the rumors she heard?

2) In your opinion, would you have declined the invitation from Mason if it would not affect your partner's love and trust in you?

3) What would you have suggested to Ruth to somehow erase her guilt of indebtedness to Otis for all his kindness showed?

4) Since Otis was financially secure, do you think he went overboard in celebrating Ruth's birthday? If yes, at which point would you have drawn the line?

5) Do you think it is okay to be sexually active with your partner after you are engaged to be married?

# PART IV

# LOVE'S REWARD

# Tapestry

*"The mind is its own place, and in itself, can make heaven of Hell, and a hell of Heaven." — John Milton*

Trying to get a feel for Otis's take on his soon-to-be new role as head of their household, and also father of her sons, Ruth held his hand close to the side of her warm breast and softly asked her love, "Baby, what do you want the boys to call you after we are married. And ...umm, do you want me to change their names?"

Smiling at his love, Otis replied, "Baby, you know I'm cool with whatever they call me...okay, let me see. Otis! Dad! It doesn't matter to me, Baby...I am fine. And if it's going to be too much hassle for you and the kids, you don't have to change their names... besides, I already consider them mine."

This was great news for Ruth, and she smiled as they continued in love. Agreeing to start making plans for the wedding that weekend, the two lovebirds left the restaurant, and Ruth headed back to work to continue her shift while Otis took the interstate highway to visit some patients of his at a health center across town. Ruth was back on time, and during her second short break, she stopped over at Naomi's room to tell her about her dinner. She couldn't spend much time with her as Edwin, Naomi's son, had stopped by to visit his mother before heading home after a board meeting he had attended. The night went by quickly for Ruth, but by the time her shift had ended, Naomi was fast asleep.

Ruth headed home to Brian and Marcus, who were up, waiting to share their day's experience with her. It was enjoyable to share those fun-filled stories, but they had to cut it short without even discussing Marcus's question earlier that morning, as the young men had to wake up early in the morning for school the next day. After the boys were in bed, Ruth went into her room, took out her wisdom journal, and updated it with what Naomi had shared with her that day. She said her prayers, called her man, and then fell asleep an hour later.

The next morning, Ruth drove her sons to school and those kids who didn't get a chance to see the two studs being dropped off in school with that Mercedes the previous day where on deck to see them that morning. Ruth, Brian, and Marcus enjoyed every moment of it. When Ruth went to work that day, she stopped over at her friend's and apologized for not having enough time to share with her the previous day.

"Hmm!" Naomi began. "I have something for you...but see me before you leave tonight...don't forget now...even if I am asleep, wake me up."

"C'mon now, you know I wouldn't do that...but I will promise to see you during each break that I take, sound good?" Ruth asked.

"Sure, Hon," Naomi replied.

Curious as to what Naomi had for her, Ruth's mind circled the globe, and each time she stopped by during her shift to get a hint as to what was in store for her, she couldn't get a squeak out of Naomi. During her third and final break, Naomi handed her a card, made Ruth promise not to open it until she got home, and most of all not to let Otis know anything about it, because it was "between us girls." Promising to be true to her word, Ruth didn't open the card, but tried to get a feel for what was enclosed. She couldn't, as it was not weighty. Maybe just a few hundred dollar bills, which she could always use? But why would Naomi not want her to open the card for that reason? Ruth put the card in her bag and went on about her business with flashes of curiosity. At the end of her shift, weary Naomi was fast asleep. The PT that was helping her hips also left her exhausted.

When Ruth got home that night, after hugs and kisses from her "stud muffins," Brian and Marcus, she ran to the bathroom, took her shower, and then rejoined the boys as they settled into bed, to find out what was in the card. It was a ritual the three of them had shared ever since Marcus was born; they would settle down and open their presents together. For Ruth, this was no different. They shared all their joys and sorrows, and like a little girl trapped in this queen's body, she was anxious and excited by Naomi's gift. So she asked Marcus to open the card, and Brian to read it.

Before Marcus could begin, Ruth said, "We need to address the question in the car from yesterday morning, remember?"

"Oh yeah," Marcus began. "I think we should call Doc 'Dad,' and change our names, so that Brian and I will have the same last name."

"Same here, Mom," Brian concurred.

"Are you guys sure that's what you want?" Ruth asked her sons.

"Yeah, Mom, Doc is cool...he is a good man," the boy remarked.

"Well, we'll all be changing our names then," Ruth said with a smile, and then continued, "So where were we?"

Marcus did the honors by opening the card as Brian and Ruth did the drum roll. There was a check and a note enclosed, so Brian gave Ruth the check, and read the note. Her eyes lit up. She hadn't seen so many zeros on a check all her life. And the note read:

*Dear Ruth,*

*Though through not the best of times and circumstances, I am glad the good Lord has allowed our paths to meet in this life. I have come to love you as my caregiver, my daughter, confidant, and friend. I have watched you grow from a woman into a lady, and again I am proud to know you as a friend. You have made this whole experience at the nursing home bearable and comfortable for me, and thank you for being the one I can turn to and cry with since I lost my, Elliot. There are so many things I wish we could share together, but with time, I know we will.*

*I thought it wise to kill two birds with one stone and therefore enclosed, you will find a check for $150,000 to help you celebrate what's left of your birthday week, and assist you with the plans for your wedding to Otis. I know you'll make a wonderful and faithful wife and mother, and I'm sure you two will have a love-filled marriage, as did Elliot and I.*

*Belated Greetings on your Birthday; and CONGRATULATIONS on your Engagement!*

*Love*
*Naomi.*
*Ps...Don't forget our promise.*

Ruth couldn't contain herself and broke down into tears. All her life she had wanted a mother and friend, and here this woman who didn't know her from Adam a few months ago was showing her so much kindness. It was as if the windows of heaven were opened, and God had commanded the angels to bless Ruth until she didn't have room enough to receive her blessings. She pulled her sons close to her and the three of them hugged. And with shattered bouts of laughter as she wiped her eyes, Ruth held her sons' hands and said: "Remember I told you, God will always come through for us if we are obedient to his commandment and treat people the way we want to be treated. It's our turn to receive, and he is not through with us as yet...and guys, about the promise I made with Mrs. Parsons, I promised not to tell Otis about this, so whatever you do, this should not leave this room, promise?"

Shaking their heads in agreement, Brian and Marcus promised not to disclose the contents of this life-changing gift their mother had received.

Before going to bed, Brian asked Ruth, "So Mom, what would you do with all this money?"

Smiling, Ruth said, "Well, I will save some for your college and I will have to use some for the wedding...not a lot...but mostly for your college. I was wondering how I could ever afford to send you two brainiacs to college, but again, God always comes through... Thank You, Jesus!" Ruth shouted.

She tickled the boys, gave each a peck on the cheek, and told them to hurry and go to sleep, and walked out the door towards her bedroom. After securing the house, saying her prayers, and thanking God for the provision, Ruth called Otis and spent about thirty minutes on the phone with him. She explained to him that she was a little exhausted from the day and that she would call him in the morning after dropping the boys off at school. He was grateful, as he also had a long day at work. After a couple of hours of sleep, Ruth was wide-eyed and couldn't get back to sleep. The parade of her thoughts about how far she had come and of God's blessings on her life kept her awake until daybreak.


That Friday, Ruth arrived early to spend some time with Naomi. She gave her a hug and said thank you for such a generous gift. Then she made the mistake of saying, "You shouldn't have."

To that, Naomi was quick to respond in a firm but softest of tone, "My dear, I know I shouldn't have, but learn this today: Whenever someone does something good for you, be it man or woman, out of the goodness of their heart, with no strings attached, the most you should say after thanking that person is, 'Thank you, Jesus.' Don't abort your blessings my dear…this is God's way of providing for you…I know you didn't mean it that way, but like I always try to guide you, when it comes to the opposite sex, take this from me: I know society has taught us to act all independent and self-sufficient, but please know this, and teach my boys, Brian and Marcus too, that such words have the power to cancel your blessings in heaven. So never say, 'you shouldn't have,' to anyone who shows you an act of kindness with no strings attached. Okay, Hon.? Now tell me, do you think this will be enough for the wedding plans, too? Larry and Edwin wanted to do more, but I explained to them that neither you nor their uncle is as flashy as they'd think. I also made them promise not to share this information with anyone I did not give birth to. That includes their wives. You see, darling, in as much as Otis can afford it all, I see myself in you, and <u>when it comes to a wedding, it should always make the bride feel much better about herself when she can contribute to the costs, and not just the groom. No matter how rich he is, your dime should be in it, too. I know some women want all for themselves, and not to spend a penny of their money, but that is wrong. You could end up losing your self-respect, and that's how some in-laws get all mixed up in weddings and marriages. There used to be a time when the bride's parents would bear the brunt of the wedding expenses. With all these changes, and one has to now guess about who the bride is, who knows anymore?"</u>

Quickly apologizing for her comment, Ruth was most grateful for her correction and appreciated her friend, who was looking out for her. Ruth and Otis had agreed to start making plans the next day, but a day earlier for her was just as great, because Naomi was all excited about her friend getting married.

Ruth would have preferred to elope, but with Naomi's kind gesture, she now had to plan a wedding in town and it had to be sizable, considering the amount. She would rather have shared her blessing with those less fortunate, especially some of the nurses at GMNH, but all she could do was to make sure she extended a hand whenever she could. She had been taught that it was more blessed to give than to receive, and so over the years, Ruth had made it a part of her life to be generous in her donations to charities. For her wedding, however, Ruth would find it difficult to cut corners and share her blessings.

Ruth's breaks that day at work were spent on the phone in Naomi's room, as they had to come up with some kind of game plan before the discussion with Otis on Saturday. She checked and compared the prices offered for a wedding planner, reception hall, and accessories for the wedding. Seeing she was making some headway with her research, Ruth decided to take a break and get a couple of classical concert tickets, benefiting the local university's art society. She wanted to treat Otis to a night out the following evening. Knowing that his evenings were usually uneventful and that his favorite genre of music was classical, Ruth decided to go ahead and purchase the tickets. When she got home that night, Ruth called Otis to inform him of the treat he was in for the following evening, but was disappointed when he told her he had already made plans for them. Knowing the value of money, the one thing Ruth hated most of all was to waste her hard-earned dollars. Otis's rejection meant her investment in the ticket was a bust, and she did not appreciate it. However, instead of flipping out on him for making plans without first communicating with her (which Ruth was aware that she was also guilty of), she took it well and calmly asked him to discuss his future intentions with her first before making plans. She also informed him that this advice would serve her well, too, as she had purchased ticket to a benefit concert at his Alma Mater. No big deal, it was water under the bridge, and love reigned supreme in this relationship.

That Saturday afternoon, after an early lunch with Brian and Marcus, Ruth and Otis gave the boys $100 each and dropped them off at the mall, where they were supposed to meet up with some classmates, hang out, and then head off to the movie theatre inside the mall. The boys would call when they were ready to come home. This usually meant sometime between 7 and 8pm. The two lovebirds then headed over to Otis's place, where they relaxed on the sofa and spent a couple of hours discussing the date, place and time for their wedding. After that, her highness was given a royal treatment, as she was introduced to some family and friends of Otis during a ten-year-old's birthday party to which they were invited. That day they resolved the general overview of the wedding plans, the number of guests, and their preferred honeymoon location. Ruth had ordered a wedding guide that was supposed to come in the following week, so they just made notes on a couple of exercise books she had brought over with her from home.

This was getting exciting for both of them, until Ruth proposed to Otis that she would pay for her wedding dress and reception, since he would be taking care of the honeymoon and the wedding. Otis was usually easygoing and in agreement with most of Ruth's ideas and suggestions, but letting her spend money on the wedding didn't sit too well with him. They had to reach a compromise where she would just take care of her wedding dress and the needs of the bridal party, and he would take care of the wedding, reception, and honeymoon. Reassuring Ruth, Otis explained that he was willing to bet that he would not be allowed to spend a dime of his money because of the family and friends in his circle.

After the birthday party, Otis drove Ruth over to GMNH, where they visited Naomi. He took the liberty of officially introducing Ruth to Naomi, as his fiancée…it was a welcome surprise to Naomi, who was appreciative of the respect Otis extended to her as the matriarch of their family.

Naomi's health was improving and she was getting restless at the nursing home, especially whenever Ruth was not around. One day while on his rounds, Naomi pulled Dr. Swift aside and told him she wanted to discuss something of importance with him but that she'd rather wait until he had finished his day work. Thinking it was about her health, Otis stopped by immediately after work, and found Naomi in tears. Worried that she might be going through some discomfort, Otis proceeded to take out a stethoscope from his brief case while asking:

"Naomi, are you in pain? Tell me what's hurting you."

"Oh, put that thing away!" said Naomi, as she explained: "I am fine…there's just so many things in my mind." Relieved that Naomi's health was not paramount, Otis closed his briefcase with the stethoscope back in its place, pulled out a chair and sat attentively to listen to Naomi as she softly cried: "You know I've grown very fond of Ruth and you two are about to get married. I will be leaving this nursing home one of these days, by the grace of God; and I don't know what life will be like going back home without Elliot and no one to care for me like Ruth. You two will probably be moving away after you get married and that just hurts, knowing I would be all alone without a friend in this world."

Trying to comfort, Naomi, Otis mentioned: "I haven't discussed this with Ruth; but I'm sure we will not be moving away since her sons are still in school. We will be around."

"Well, can I move in with you and Ruth when you get married?" Naomi asked.

"That will be great, but my home is not wheelchair accessible and I don't think Ruth's home is either."

With a look of disappointment on Naomi's face, there was a brief silence as she weighed her alternatives. Then propping herself up on her bed, wide-eyed, she gave Otis a firm look and asked: "Do you mean to tell me that after you get married and Ruth is pregnant, you would let your wife be going up and down those stairs; and you claim to love her?"

"Well, well, umm no," Otis replied, as he wondered about the solution that would be accommodating to a pregnant Ruth.

"Well then," Naomi continued, "you will have to build her a new home in which she wouldn't have all those stairs to navigate. You don't have much time so start the ball rolling, and let me know if you need anything. And make sure you include a room for me in the design. Again, let me know if you need anything. Okay."

"I wasn't planning on it, but I will work on it. However, about the moving in with us, I think you would want to talk to Larry and Edwin about that; and also, I would have to discuss this idea with Ruth," Otis conceded.

"No, no, no...let's make the new home a surprise to Ruth. And don't let Larry and Edwin in on it either. It's just between you and me," Naomi reasoned, with a smile across her lips.

"Well, how should I discuss you moving in with us if I am not going to be telling her about the new house?" Otis asked.

"Don't worry, the new house is supposed to be a surprise gift to Ruth after you are married. It's not a secret; just a surprise...and it will be a welcomed surprise to her. You should feel guilty if it is a secret, but not when it is a surprise. Like the car, that was a surprise! Okay, better still, let's not worry about me moving in with you...I will move back home and try to work something out with Larry and Edwin to see if Ruth can leave the nursing home and be my caretaker after I am discharged, so we can be spending our daytime together. That way, Ruth doesn't have to be working this late shift anymore. You, in the meantime, will discuss our conversation with Ruth, but without the new home, right?" Naomi asked, as she smiled at Otis, knowing her brilliant plan could work.

After a minute of thought, Otis replied, "Let me think about it before bringing it to Ruth. I don't want Ruth to feel trapped or coerced into anything."

"Alright. Hurry, though, because your big day is fast approaching," Naomi concluded.

This was somewhat troubling for Otis, but he kept it to himself and gave it a long, hard thought before presenting Ruth with the idea of leaving the nursing home and just working with Naomi over at her house.

Ruth replied, "Are you kidding me? I would love it…just me and Naomi all day, and I don't have to work late…and still getting paid? Sign me up! She had mentioned something like that before, but I didn't think anything of it…since I am not about to lose my benefits with these boys still in school."

Relieved by Ruth's response, Otis's mind started racing as to what part he could play in making both ladies happy.

The next day at work, Ruth and Naomi huddled up and discussed how best to make this work in both of their favors. The solution, according to "the architect," was that Ruth would go over to Naomi's house after dropping the boys off at school in the morning, and the two would be together until the boys got off from school. Ruth would then make sure the boys were settled at home, or she could bring them over to Naomi's, where they would do their homework and stay until after dinner, and then return home for the day at about 6pm. On nights and weekends, a home health aide nurse would come in and care for Naomi. That way, she would not be without care. This was not quite good for Ruth, as she figured she would be putting in more than forty hours per week doing this running. But on the flip side, Naomi was easygoing, this would be less stressful for her, and she could use this time to plan for her wedding. Ruth would work from 8am to 6pm, and the home health aide would work from 7pm to 8am, with an hour-and-a-half lunch. Ruth would still maintain her pay scale and benefits offered at the nursing home, as she would still be employed by GMNH, but just not reporting there for duty, per the special arrangements made by Larry and Edwin with the administration and its board.

Brian and Marcus loved this arrangement, as it meant spending more time with their mom and Otis. Naomi, who could now move around quite well, was discharged the following week, and Ruth's reassignment commenced. Since the boys could take care of themselves after school, Ruth was free to spend the whole day with Naomi, and she loved it. The home health nurse was not Naomi's favorite, but she appreciated her services as she helped clean around the house, while Ruth was basically responsible for taking care of Naomi. From the first day, they were out shopping and visiting spots that Naomi and Elliot used to frequent. Ruth drove Naomi's Dodge Ram van, which was large enough to accommodate the wheelchair, and the two were usually worn out by 3pm. It was fun for Naomi, and Ruth enjoyed it, too. The two ladies were court buddies who laughed and joked all day long.

Otis loved Brian and Marcus as his own, and the three men were inseparable, to the point that sometimes, Ruth wished she had a daughter with whom she could hang out and do some fun stuff. Her sons were growing up into fine gentlemen, and their choice of profession was Otis's. He exposed the boys to the finer things in life and even took them to some local medical seminars, where he introduced them as his sons.

# The Guide

The next nine months that followed was a trying time for the couple. Romantically, Ruth was tempted to yield as a slave to her impulses, but she stood strong with support from Otis and Naomi. She rehearsed the wisdom of Naomi, while Otis endured his urges. The guest list became a moving goal post, as the couple thought of old colleague and acquaintances they wanted to introduce to each other and invite to their wedding. The wedding hall kept changing with significant increases in the number of guests, and Otis's home was fast becoming a storage bin for all the wedding and party accessories.

The saving grace in all this anxiety was the love Otis and Ruth shared, and their expectation of being together as man and wife. They would have scheduled an earlier date, but wanted the boys to be out of school and staying over at Naomi's while the couple was away on their honeymoon. Arrangements were made for Ruth's pastor to preside over the ceremony. The reception hall was booked at the Four Seasons. The wedding planner, caterer, string quintet, and musicians were all on board. The honeymoon was booked for a seven-day stay at one of the two Royal Towers of Paradise Island's Atlantis Resort in the Bahamas, and the wedding invitations were sent out well in advance. Naomi even had Ruth do a trial run three weeks before her big day, to make sure her full ensemble was in place and also that her wedding party was prepared for the day that the faucet of her tear ducts would release its flow — but this time, for joy in love.

The only issue that almost tore the couple apart was Otis's suggestion that they invite Brenda to the wedding. This opened old wounds and got Ruth a little upset.

"Why would you want to do that to me on My Day?" she asked.

"It's my day too, you know, and she is a coworker of ours. You can't invite everyone else and not her. I don't know all of these people you're inviting, but I trust you and I am willing to enjoy the day with them, so why not Brenda?" Otis responded.

"Oh! Now you want to enjoy the day with her, huh? Okay, fine!" Ruth retorted as she stormed out of the room, onto the veranda to avoid blowing a lid in fury.

Otis caught up to her. With Ruth drowning in her thoughts, with a heavy heart and tear-filled eyes, she viewed the city skyline from

Otis's veranda. Coming up behind her, Otis apologetically said, "Okay, Babe, I am sorry, but if you wanted to show the world that you are getting married, won't you want them to be there to see you in your beauty and envy the ground you walk on? Huh, Sweet Cheeks?" Then he tickled her, which got a smile out of Ruth. She turned around to share a passionate kiss.

She agreed, and Brenda was invited to the wedding and reception. The next workday, Ruth came in early and handed Brenda the invitation and told her how much she would appreciate it if she could be there; and it was delivered with a warm smile normally expected between girlfriends.

Ruth's wedding party was in place with three bridesmaids, a flower girl, and a maid of honor. A sad truth for Ruth was that she did not have any mature male figure in her life to give her away. This haunted her for the longest time, and so Naomi volunteered to act in this stead.

"After all, who knows you any better than I do?" Naomi asked.

The boys were already taller than their mom, so Brian was to walk Ruth down the aisle, and then give her hand to Marcus, who in turn would present her to Naomi. Otis's wedding party included a groomsman, three best men, who included Larry and Edwin, and a ring bearer.

A week prior to the wedding, Naomi took the time to impart some words of wisdom to Ruth, who was most receptive as she wanted above all things that her marriage would survive the challenges of life and that she would mature in love as Naomi had done throughout her life together with Elliot.

Early one afternoon while the two were out, Naomi turned to her friend and asked, "Why do you want to get married? I know you are happy with Otis, he is good to you and your sons, but why do you really want to get married? Is it all about what you can get from your partner, or is it because of love? Most people would be quick to say, it's because of love, so what is love to you, Ruth? What is love? Is it about sex, about waking up next to someone, about what your partner could provide for you, about how your partner makes you feel, or is it about love?"

Feeling a little perplexed about the nature of the questions, and wondering why Naomi at this eleventh hour in the relationship would pose such questions, Ruth simply replied, "It's because I love him. For once in my life, I am confident that I am truly in love with someone who is also in love with me."

Smiling at her friend's calculated response, Naomi continued. "You know, Ruth, generally speaking men are not too gifted at explaining things, talking, and discussing detailed issues, so be careful in this area. <u>With most men I've met, when you ask them what they are thinking about during a spell of silence, they would often reply, 'Nothing.' It is the place of that special and caring person in one's life to get them to talk. Communication is key in any relationship, and you definitely want an open line of communication in</u>

your marriage if it is to blossom. If you don't like certain things or what he tries to get you to your station, if you know what I mean, let him know it. Don't frustrate yourself and make him feel like less of a man. Communicate! Communicate! Remember this: it's not about walking down the aisle. Ask yourself: 'Is the love we share worth fighting for?' If yes, then give it all you've got, and that means even when the chips are down. Don't sweat the 'small stuff,' my dear. If you know he loves you and his world revolves around you, don't sweat the small stuff. Go with what you know and not how you feel. He may not be able to express his love for you from time to time, but your happiness is primary to him. So don't throw your cereal in the trash because you can't find a toy in the box…it was meant to fill you, not tickle you.

"Baby?" Naomi continued. "Marriage is a major life-altering process. Before you and Otis walk down that aisle, ask yourself: 'What will I do or how will I ensure that my marriage is not like the others that have ended up in divorce?' You have to be willing to die to your flesh in order to make it work. Are you willing to die to your flesh, Ruth? Are you? Most people so doggedly go after their partner, trying to appease their flesh when God has called us to die to it. Total submission, Ruth, total submission. A man should totally submit to God and his wife, and a woman should totally submit to God and her husband for this thing to work. Some of our parents lived in marriage for years and they were miserable and unhappy, but they remained together because they decided to co-exist with each other. That's not what marriage is, Ruth…it should be filled with joy, happiness, fruitfulness, and most of all, love.

"You see, marriage is not supposed to be a union between a man and a woman…it is a triple bottom-line, an iron triangle, and a three-fold cord that is not easily broken. It is supposed to be a union between God, a man, and his wife. But couples usually leave God out of the equation and constantly wonder why things are not working out right. I don't mean to preach to you, Ruth, but the Bible clearly tells us that if we seek God first, his kingdom, and his righteousness, then everything else will be added to us or come in line with our desire, which is now godly. We always tend to overlook this passage of scripture, but in all reality, it is the key to prosperous living. This means that before you talk to the man, talk to God. And before you seek to please the man, seek to please God. I guarantee you that if you make this a practice, your marriage will live forever and you will have joy, happiness, fruitfulness, and love in it.

"I know Otis loves and cares for you and your sons dearly, but be careful with how you manage your finances when you two get married. Yes, a man should be the provider of the home, but don't let him do all the spending…and don't make what's his, yours, and what's yours, yours either. Also, don't try to be the financial warden. He needs a helpmeet, not a manager. Give him some latitude in what and how he spends. You two have to not only love, but also respect each other. If love abides, look out and care for your partner — and if you have children, your family — making sure they lack nothing should be your burden and first priority. So spending on self should really be a secondary issue if your priorities are in order. Challenge each other in love when it comes to caring for your mate and partner through wise spending and making sure you are comfortable in your finances. Iron sharpeneth iron, my dear. You shouldn't be making decisions about purchases concerning the entire family, or let me say big ticket items, without consulting with each other. Some men would relinquish that responsibility to their wives. But even if they do, always remember to let them know what's going on with the purchases. I understand that sometimes we would see something in the store that we need for ourselves even though we are on a budget. That is fine. Just don't overdo it. Don't try to keep up with the Joneses or be in trend with fashion while your home is suffering. You see, finances are one of the leading causes of separation and divorces in marriages, so be on your guard.

"If the tides of time should change and you become the bread winner or main provider in the family, even though you two agree to tighten your belt and spend less, based on the reduction of your income, remember to still treat him with love and respect. Be liberal to him as he was to you when he was the main provider. This will be hard for some women to stomach, but it's true. A fair percentage of successful women are having a hard time keeping their marriages or maintaining relationships, all because they don't know how to treat people, not just their partner, with respect, when success is on their side. If you should ever get to the stage of financial independence and success in life, don't try to rub your partner's face in it or have a prideful look and attitude about you. Ruth, promise me you will always treat people the way you want to be treated."

To this Ruth earnestly responded, as she was engrossed in the wisdom of her friend.

"Some people claim that men are intimidated by successful women. However, I wouldn't call it intimidation on the part of men. You see, just as we have this innate yearning to nurture, and without a child some of us go through depression, likewise, men have a burning desire to provide. When that is taken away or they cannot fulfill this role, most feel useless in the relationship or marriage no matter what other contribution they make. So be understanding. I am sure you wouldn't want your mate to talk down to you because you can't bear a child or can't cook too well. So, be mindful of how you treat people.

"Sometimes we as people — I don't know why — tend to belittle our spouses in front of our relatives and friends, and men are particularly guilty of this. I really don't know if we are ashamed of our partners or we just think that by putting them down, we are elevating our status in the eyes of our audience. That is so wrong. If you can't speak favorably or respectfully of the person in your life, how would you expect the world to see them in a more favorable and respectable light? Be careful, because when you point one finger, three are pointing back at you. And besides, a man is known by the company he or she keeps. Birds of the same feather flock together. So if you talk about him like a 'dog' when around your family or friends, guess what? In reality, they will see you as a 'bitch.' If your home doesn't sell you, the streets won't buy you…so without going into your personal life, always make sure you present your partner in a respectable and favorable way, because it is a direct reflection on you as a person and an indictment on the integrity of your character.

"Also, never compare your relationship or marriage with someone else's, no matter how hard they try to convince you that their love is second to none. You don't know what's going on behind closed doors, what sacrifices they've made to have what they claim is golden, or even if they are lying. So be careful, Honey. The devil can use those aspirations for perfection to bring defeat to what you have been praying for and once thought was a blessing. It can lead to despair, depression, and not to mention separation or even a divorce. The grass isn't always greener on the other side, my dear, and no two relationships or marriages are the same, okay? You'll have a hard enough time trying to keep yours together, so don't try to emulate what someone else wants you to think. Trust me, I know what I'm talking about. If not for the grace of God, I could have messed up my marriage trying to mold my family in the likeness of my dear Aunt Mildred's. And later I came to find out that I had cousins she was not even aware of.

"Concerning Otis's friends — as much as both you and Otis would want you as his wife to always be a gracious hostess, try not to be too close or overfriendly with them. Do you understand, honey? Otis's friends may treat and see him as a 'brother,' but don't get it twisted. They are most likely not looking at you as a 'sister,' no matter how innocent it looks. That doesn't mean you have to be rude…just be on your guard and draw the line early with everyone he invites into your home and around your family. Okay?

"Another thing, Baby. Keep your family circle tightly close… watch out for the so-called 'friends,' and mind not to put the things you discuss as a family out in the street. You can lose your partner's trust and love if you can't keep your mouth shut or are flippant about things that are trusted to your hearing only. Some women are trapped in what I call the 'age of relief'…it is the age one loses her innocence and discusses it with a confidant or close one. The relief felt in the release of information is subconsciously sought after by perpetuating the sharing of both personal and non-personal information. It can be at any age. It can come from a girls' night out, a pajama party, a sleepover, or even a mere time spent together with a close friend or loved one. This cycle, if you are not careful, can continue into adulthood. All of a sudden, you find yourself innocently sharing personal information with a friend or family member about your partner or husband, about his size, his tendencies, what design of underwear he prefers, his likes and dislikes…thereby, again, you've innocently established an image of your husband in your friends' minds…causing them to recreate your experience in their minds and what they would have done to enhance the experience if they were in your position. God help you, if they are not satisfied with what they have. That's why we hear of a mother sleeping with her son-in-law, sister sleeping with brother-in-law, friend going after friend's husband or wife...all because the wife or girlfriend couldn't keep her intimate life to herself. Be careful, my dear...always remember that your personal business is your personal business...not anyone else's.

"Sometimes, Ruth, Otis will ask you to do something for him that you both know he can do for himself. Yes, we are all busy and he is not in kindergarten, however, be there for him regardless of how trivial his request seems. It could be for something as simple as making a few calls or even fixing a button. For a good number of men, difficult tasks are seen as a challenge which they'd gladly conquer, but it's the routine or mundane things in life that trip them. So be on your guard. Look at the big picture before negative thoughts dictate your attitude.

"Honey, you two are about to take your vows in the sight of God and man, and one thing I would advise you to do is to make sure you both absolutely agree that divorce is not an option, come hell or high water, before you walk down that aisle. You have to be willing to stand forever, or you will not be standing very long. I know Otis won't have a problem with this, but make sure that you both share chores around the house. There's no such thing as a man's job or a woman's job. A man of character would not want to see or hear that his wife is doing any manual labor, but at the same time, offer to help...let him tell you 'no'...which I know most men will do. But still, offer your assistance. I know Brian and Marcus are old enough to take care of a lot of stuff, but this could also be good quality time to share, when the two of you work together.

"If for whatever reason there is a strain in the relationship and you don't like what you are getting back, always first check what you are giving. Again, make 1 Corinthians 13 the essence of the love you share in your marriage. Like life, marriage will come with ebbs and flows…but like the northern star, my dear, be constant in love. Don't let the good or the not-so-good times breed discontent.

"Again, be creative and take turns to come up with stuff to do in having quality time. Never stop dating and having fun with each other after you get married…it is very important. Keep not just love, but your friendship alive. The boys will soon be off to college, so make sure that they see an example of true love in your marriage before they leave…it will guide them in their expectations. Darling, you know you are beautiful and you will be getting a lot of unwanted attention, as will Otis, but remember not to put yourself in any position where your body is speaking louder than your mind. Don't indulge in flirting with men — and these days, women too — and disrespect your husband, your home, and yourself. Be careful about the programs or shows you watch and listen to. These can feed your spirit negatively or positively…remember, you are what you eat. When you come to the fork in the road where life hands you a choice, always remember to make your decisions based on the word of God. Try not to ever settle for a permanent or long-term solution to a temporary situation. I shouldn't be telling you this. You are a lady, so whatever you do, make sure it's done in moderation, and be content with what the Lord has blessed you. Contentment is great gain, my dear.

"Another thing: don't make the mistake some wives make, thinking that now that they are married they can relax and not tend to their affairs. By that, I mean please continue keeping your home clean. You don't have to be all obsessive about it, but keep it neat and clean. It's both you and your man's castle, and the place he should be longing for and running to, in order to get some relief and rest. Don't put him in a position where he has to think twice before coming home or inviting a guest over.

"Also, don't get yourself frustrated over petty stuff, like the way he places the toilet tissue or him leaving the toilet seat up or even him not always wanting to go out and do stuff on a day he'd like to rest. Some of us think that Saturdays and Sundays are for running all over the world. Based on your partner's background, those two days could mean days of rest from a hectic week. So try to understand each other and make compromises while you are courting, instead of one person feeling that their world is being run ragged, while the other feels they've just stepped into the sleep zone. I guess what I am trying to say, Ruth, is not to major on the less busy or minor things in life. There are far more hair-raising issues that deserve your attention than some of these petty issues I've seen couples get divorced over. No matter how upset or angry you get, don't go to bed mad at each other. Also, don't abuse each other physically or emotionally over a difference of opinion, because you will not always agree with each other's point of view. When you hurt each other, and you are still together, guess who will have to suffer from the broken heart and wounded spirit…you! Our actions have more far-reaching implications than we'd like to think. They affect not just us and those around us. So, be on your guard and resolve your differences amicably, and not out of malice or hatred because someone else doesn't share your point of view.

"As a couple, try not to keep secrets from each other. I am telling you, that breeds deceitfulness. Share your life and moments with him and consciously erase every situation that will lead to distrust and doubts. And try not to exclude one another from each other's social activities. Leave some room for common sense. Let your partner decide not to get involved and don't discourage him from being a part of something you enjoy. For example, as a lady — I know this would sound silly to some — don't exclude or discourage your husband from, let's say, joining your knitting club. Common sense and manhood would have taught him that he shouldn't be everywhere doing everything with you. Likewise, as a wife, your husband shouldn't discourage or exclude you from joining him at, let's say, a hunting or fishing trip with his friends. Common sense and virtuous wisdom should have taught you not to trail him or be everywhere he is, because you have his heart. Furthermore, don't try to drag your partner into something you think he 'should' enjoy with you. Never force anyone to please you. Love is the key, my dear. Love is the key. If you and the marriage or relationship means more to your partner, he will want to be where you are; not just to please you, but because it brings peace to his soul. Trust in each other's commitment to the marriage. Faith and wisdom in love should be your guiding light as you progress."

The whole week was full of words of wisdom from Naomi as Ruth confessed to her friend that she had been keeping a wisdom journal of all the things she had been taught since the Lord brought their paths together. Naomi admonished Ruth not to take her husband for granted; a tendency in humans when getting comfortable with someone.

Naomi continued: "Appreciate him for who he is, not what you'd like him to become. We sometimes try to change our partners into something and someone else after we've become complacent with the person we fell in love with. Isn't it funny how when most men get married, they prefer their wives to stay the same way they were when they were dating, while most women try all they can to change their husband into the vision they have of who he should be in their eyes? You see, Ruth, your husband is not your girlfriend, so don't try to treat him as one. And don't try to dress him like one, either. It's cute, but not becoming of a man. He is a pace-setter and a leader. Don't try to usurp his authority or be the pack leader, especially when in public. He may not say anything, but don't think it went unnoticed if that ever happened. Which I pray will not, in your case. He is also a burden bearer and will stand strong for you and his family when the chips are down…you just have to let him fulfill his role. This is something we as women are guilty of doing…trying to protect the men in our lives from standing in the gap. We end up making sissies of our sons and impotent men of our husbands. Let him fulfill his role as a lover, a friend, a father, brother, and husband.

"I know I have told you this before, but try not to emasculate him in the way you treat him and what you say to him, no matter how upset you get. Life's trials will come your way and it is up to you two to decide if you will let these trials tear you apart or bring you closer. And trust me, you will get upset…no one is perfect…it takes the grace of God to live a long time with someone under the same roof. You two need to complement each other. Your weaknesses should be his strength, and vice versa. A husband and wife shouldn't be tearing each other apart because of their apparent weaknesses. That's really not nice…no one is perfect. Make sure you elevate each other in each other's eyes and the eyes of the world. You also want to respect each others' privacy…don't be reading his mail and going through his stuff…no one would want someone else to do that to them.

"A man who knows his purpose is also a fighter, a guide, a guard, and a pillar of strength, meaning he has a calming presence about him. He will fight for you emotionally, physically, spiritually, and in whatever arena his love is challenged. You see, he loves his wife as he loves himself, and will take things personally whenever he perceives that his love is being challenged. But baby, all these attributes can be erased with constant criticism and nagging…you don't want to do that. Never worry about the things you can't change, or try to change things that don't go your way by degrading the love you have and share with your husband. That's not the way of love, and neither should a man treat the woman in his life in such a manner.

"Ruth, a man is also a problem solver. Even if it comes to mechanical stuff or things you both know he is not familiar with, let him try…don't belittle him by telling him what he knows he can't do. Suggest that he call an expert, and reason with him that you two can have more time to spend together if he can get someone else to complete the task. They always fall for that. You see, honey, it's all about the way you communicate to the love in your life. Bottom line: treat him the way you'd like to be treated. With all I've said, the underlying fact is that you have to be consistently committed in all you do. Be committed to communicating with your spouse — and by that I mean listen attentively, and not just hear what he has to say. Be committed to love, committed to resolving your tiffs or conflicts amicably, committed to learning more about your spouse and even yourself. Yep, you heard right — yourself. Some of us don't know much about ourselves, I'm ashamed to say. And most of all, be committed to romance. Be romantic and keep the fire burning, honey. Walk with your head held high…know who you are and whose you are. If you have the love of God and your spouse, don't be afraid of nay sayers or the enemy…perfect love casteth out fear. Be confident in your love; but not prideful, okay? In times of difficulties, always remember that God is willing and able; and that he has you in the palms of his hands. In fact, when you've settled down this evening, read Isaiah 49: 14-16. That's one of my favorite verses of scripture."

"Ruth, I have seen the humility with which you have served me and listened to my every word since we met. I know this whole week I have been beating you over the head with all these cautions, but I trust you will do what's right, and I know that the love both you and Otis share will stand the tests of time. I am proud of you, Ruth. I see you as my daughter, and there is no greater satisfaction for a mother than to know that she has instilled in her daughter the best of values," Naomi finished, as she hugged her friend in tears.

# The Wedding

*"Reexamine all that you have been told in school, or in church or in any book. Dismiss whatever insults your soul."* — Walt Whitman

On June 24th the following year, Ruth Moore and Otis Swift invited 650 guests to share in the joy of the beginning of their new life together when they exchanged their marriage vows. The wedding planner did a wonderful job in decorating the church; enveloped in the scent of fresh summer flowers with pink, ivory and sky blue ribbons and bows adorning each entrance to the church, its dark brown pews and window ceils. The wedding ceremony was great and you should have seen your girl, Ruth. She had her hair in ballerina bun with pearl-floral hair wire, and a set of pearl earrings. Ruth was in a custom, ivory, classic wedding gown, with cathedral floor-length train, satin lining, much beading work and boning with detailed embroidered chiffon outside, and a veil that complemented her gown. Ruth looked amazing, graceful, and absolutely heavenly with her soft and radiant face, her natural glow accentuated with a barely noticeable makeup. She was beauty personified, a vision of perfection that only God could create. The bridal party was also elegantly dressed, with the bridesmaids wearing custom-made gorgeous embroidered chiffon pink dresses satin lining. Brian and Marcus had on their single-breasted three-button black tuxes, with sparkling white shirts, maroon bow ties, and cummerbunds and looked very sharp. Otis and his wedding party had on back single-breasted three-button black tuxes. He had on a beige cummerbund and bow tie, while the rest of his groomsman and best men were in silver. Naomi, the queen mother, was elegantly attired and looked the part with a beige lace and iridescent chiffon strapless Mon Cheri ball gown, hand-beaded bodice, full skirt with circular cascading ruffles, and matching shawl. She knew she looked great.

Otis and his party took their places as the crowded sanctuary lost its collective breath at the sight of Ruth gliding down the aisle on Brian's arm. She looked absolutely heavenly and Otis was nervous with pride, joy, and disbelief, just thinking about how blessed he was and how long it took him to find true love.

Ruth couldn't believe it either, that for all she had gone through in life, there was still a man who was sincere enough to wait for her at the end of the aisle. The ceremony was simply elegant, starting with a string quintet that provided a remarkable selection of classical and contemporary music such as Handel's *Arrival of the Queen of Sheba,* and Shania Twain's *From this Moment,* which captivated the congregation's attention. Ending with the preacher's word of exhortation, there was not a stone left unturned in trying to match the simple yet sophisticated beauty of the couple. Cued by the minister, wedding bands were exchanged, and the two exchanged their vows, which they each chose to write. Ruth was the first one up. With eyes filled with love and fixed on Otis's, she said:

*"Otis, I had to wait in line for love and prayed it wouldn't run dry*

*And every time I looked ahead someone else was satisfied*

*While still in line, I saw the faces of those who passed me by*

*Some full of laughter and of love; and others asking why*

*It was a long wait, I must admit, and sometimes I even cried.*

*Now it's my turn; nervous, I close my eyes, stretch out my hands, and here you are.*

*Otis, I love you with all my heart*

*I have come to see you as love; and a gift from above*

*I may not be many things, but this much I do know*

*That I will give you all my love and be faithful through it all*

*I will stand by your side and be your wife, lover, and friend*

*And I will give all I've got and do whatever is best for you.*

*If later down life's path you should ever wonder why, or how we make it through,*

*Just know that in this world and the next,*

*This day, I resign my love to you.*

*I love you, Otis, and I always will."*

Otis was all in tears when it became his turn. With quivering hands and trembling lips, the groom stated:

*"Ruth, I can remember, for it was like yesterday.*

*I was doing my rounds with my head buried in a patient's chart, when you walked by.*

*Somehow I had to raise my head to see who it was who made time stand still.*

*Ever since then, there has never been a day that's gone by without me thinking of you.*

*Through the dark times in my life you were still the glimmer of hope*

*That maybe one day love will come my way*

*I have since come to love and appreciate you as a very attractive and beautiful lady, and most of all, a virtuous woman.*

*Ruth, I know I am privileged to stand right here with you today*

*And God in his mercy and on my behalf has matched our lives as one*

*I wish I could find the words to express how much I love and care for you.*

*The closest I can come is that I love you with every fiber of my being, and I will forever love you.*

*I pledge my love to you today and to you and you alone*

*I will forever do my very best to treat you like a lady and a queen.*

*I will honor and respect you and as long as I live*

*I will be true to you*

*And will always love you, Ruth."*

By this time, half the congregation was teary-eyed and the other half were wishing they were as much in love as Otis and Ruth. Of everyone present, no one beamed with pride as much as Naomi. The ceremony continued in love, after which the wedding party recessed to the entrance of the church, where a dozen white doves were released into the open skies, and confetti showered on the couple. It was a beautiful sunny day, in the low seventies, with a slight breeze, and clear skies. The wedding party then proceeded to a nearby pristine lake, where they took the most memorable pictures celebrating Ruth and Otis's day.

A couple of hours later that afternoon, the wedding party headed to the reception hall gorgeously decorated with white and red carnations and roses, which was now filled with family and friends, all waiting to share this moment with the couple.

The reception hall was sprinkled with a scent of beautiful soft perfume that invited the guests to take another gentle sniff; while guarded by cream-colored walls conservatively designed with pink and sky blue waves of ribbons. Also admirable was the seamless flow of the whole event and the seating arrangements, as requested by Otis and Ruth. The wedding party was seated at the front of the hall in a semi-circular arrangement with the bride and groom in the middle. Between the wedding party and the guests was an open space that could be transformed into a dancing stage.

Covered in 96-inch round white polyester linens, each table had in place: heart-shaped ceramic dinner plates with matching cutleries, pearlized shell place card holders, interlocking heart candle holder, personalized champagne flutes and personalized: matchbooks, napkins, ribbons, fans and parasols, pens and notepads, candies, and coasters for each seated guest. On the side, visible to everyone, was a table hosting a classic four-tiered white butter cream and marble cake, iced with off-white fondant, beautifully decorated with scroll-work, and topped with a cluster of cream flowers, guarded by a glittery cake knife and server set.

The reception commenced with a prayer from the pastor and was followed by toasts from the groomsman, the maid of honor, and Naomi.

Trying to keep it short and sweet, Naomi began with a call to attention and then on her feet, she remarked:

*"I want to take this opportunity to thank everyone for affording Otis and Ruth this time on such a beautiful day. I have known Otis since he was a boy and I have watched him grow into one of the finest men my eyes have ever seen. He is a brilliant physician, a gentleman, and most of all, a man of God. I have come to know Ruth as my daughter and friend. She is a beautiful lady, the mother of two very handsome and intelligent young men and most of all, a woman of God. I was married once and know what it means to love and be loved. Otis and Ruth are in love with each other.*

*"We sometimes keep crying to God to send us an answer even after he's assured us that no good thing will he withhold from us, that he will supply all our needs according to his riches in glory, by Christ Jesus; and that whatsoever we shall ask in his name, believing, we shall receive. You see, over the years, I have come to realize that God always puts the answer in place before the problem arises...he*

*said he is a very present help, and while we are yet speaking he will hear. And so I ask you to rise to your feet and join me in thanking God for Otis, Ruth's answer; and Ruth, Otis's answer. To Ruth and Otis! Thank You, God!"*

It was a very enjoyable time. Ruth tossed her bouquet to a group of single ladies, each waiting with anticipation to catch the gorgeous ring of wide-open peonies and tulips encircling a cluster of barely open pink, white, and red roses. Otis tossed the garter, a wide strip of organza, accented with a crisp satin bow, to the single men. The couple danced to Luther Vandross's *Hear and Now* as their selection. The music included Disco, Motown, and line dancing. The cake was cut and shared, and flashes went off all throughout the reception from cameras of the guests and that of the official wedding photographer.

Around 7:30pm, Otis and Ruth said goodbye to the guests, Naomi, and their sons, then left for the airport, where a private jet owned by one of his friends was waiting to take the couple to their honeymoon at the Atlantis Resort in the Bahamas. Their suitcases were already on board, and they let out a sigh of relief when they were finally airborne.

However, this was a bittersweet moment for Ruth, as this was the first time she would be leaving Brian and Marcus for such a long period of time. However, she knew they would be safe and happy with Naomi while she and Otis were away. By the time the newly-weds checked in to their suite, after more than four hours of flight, they were exhausted. Otis and Ruth both knew he couldn't carry her over the threshold, so he didn't even pretend or try. Mr. and Mrs. Swift kissed, undressed each other and showered together before the exhaustion got the better of them. They were fast asleep soon after their heads hit the pillows. At about 6:00 am, after a short rest, the fireworks were in play…and worth the wait.

While the couple was away on their honeymoon, Brian and Marcus grew taller and heavier from all the leftovers they had from the wedding celebrations. They enjoyed their time with Naomi and were at her beck and call while she told them inspiring stories of her adolescent years, and how Larry and Edwin navigated their academic years in excellence. The boys anticipated Naomi's every need, and the three of them hung out during the day and watched TV together until late each night.

# The Mansion

*"The greatest discovery of our generation is that human beings can alter their lives by altering their attitudes of mind. As you think, so shall you be." — William James*

R uth and Otis were hand in glove with each other, and the love they shared emitted positive energy to all at the resort. They had a wonderful and relaxing time together, and more than made up for their celibate period. While on the island, Ruth called a couple of times to check up on Brian, Marcus, and Naomi. All was well, which put her mind at ease to enjoy her honeymoon.

The living arrangements after the marriage were that Ruth would sell her home or lease it out. She and the boys would start moving in with Otis the week of their return from their honeymoon. His was a safer and more reserved neighborhood.

The Sunday afternoon after their return from the honeymoon, Otis drove his wife over to a new development about fifteen minutes away from Naomi's home. Ruth thought they were going to visit a friend or relative of his to express their appreciation for their participation or attendance at the wedding. Otis pulled into the driveway of the most beautiful home in the development. However, all the blinds were down.

Switching off the engine, Otis turned to his wife and said, "Mrs. Swift, I know you were supposed to start moving over tomorrow. However, I think you deserve better...so here you are. This is your new home." Reaching across to stunned Ruth, he gave her a soft kiss on the lips, handed her a set of keys, and said, "Okay, let's go see where we will be living."

This was all too much for Ruth, as she never in her wildest dreams thought of herself, as a new bride, moving into a brand new home. After a minute of shaking her head in disbelief, Ruth muttered, "And you are not kidding?"

To which Otis replied, "Not when it comes to my love for you, Baby...c'mon, let's go see our new home."

As the couple walked towards the front door of their single floor contemporary Tudor model home with marble stone walls, Ruth's mind was already at 2,500 RPM. She was thinking about flowers to enhance her home's exterior, and designs to give it more curb appeal, a result of her watching HGTV channel one time too many. Ruth then handed Otis the keys to the house; and opening the door, Ruth was greeted by the smell of new designer paint and carpet and welcomed by the security alarm that heralded the queen home. Otis disabled the alarm, and told Ruth that the code was the date of their first date. The interior walls were painted with soft colors and overlooked by two twenty-bulb chandeliers at the hallway and in the living room.

Ruth and Otis walked around the house as he inspected every detail of the finishing touches the architect and builders were supposed to include in the design. Noticing he was all alone on one side of the house, Otis retraced his steps and found Ruth in the living room. With brightened eyes full of excitement, Ruth was in a world of her own as she soliloquized about color schemes, drapes, décor, lighting and rugs. A walk into the kitchen filled with the scent of unwrapped amenities didn't help either when the couple resumed their tour; especially after seeing the island unit that included a sink, cabinets for storage, granite counters, a stovetop, a warming oven, and a small refrigerator. *Whoa! I could even entertain in this kitchen. It's as if Otis had invited a celebrity designer to stop by and model the perfect kitchen for me. Wow!* Ruth thought as she added to her excitement.

The five bedrooms and four-and-a-half baths were all spacious. The master bedroom had a master bath that included a Jacuzzi, and a veranda overlooking the backyard. Included in this mini mansion was a full basement; media room; study; a four-car garage; a sun room; a quarter-acre fenced-in back yard with an in-ground swimming pool; and a bonus room. Whenever Otis walked out of a room Ruth was inspecting and admiring, upon his return, he had an appreciative kiss.

Taking a break from the endless stream of ideas, Ruth asked Otis, "So when did you get the time to get all this done?"

"I must admit, I have Naomi to thank and her input was invaluable...she actually picked out most of these appliances, features, and styles," Otis replied.

After another appreciative kiss, while in each other's arms, Ruth softly said to her husband: "Honey, you know that I love you with all my heart, right? I truly appreciate all you have done for me...and I know you love and care not just for me, but for Brian and Marcus also...so darling, don't take this the wrong way, okay? Baby, I don't want you to spend another cent on this family for the next six months...please, please? I will furnish the home and take care of any bill that comes up...I just don't want you to spend, for now, please?"

"Okay! Honey, that's no problem, really," Otis replied. "Trust me if I couldn't, I wouldn't...I want to do everything for you, Brian and Marcus...you are my family now, and you shouldn't lack for anything."

"I know, Baby," Ruth continued. "But I want to do this, I really do...please? Let me contribute, okay, Hon?" Taking a deep sigh, she admitted. "Sweetie, I have a little confession to make, now that we are married. Please don't get upset."

"Baby, I won't. What is it?" Otis asked as he gently lowered himself to the floor, sitting with his back to the wall and arms folded across his arched knees.

"Well!" Ruth began, as she nestled next to her husband. "Baby, you know I am not from a wealthy family and neither do I have some kind of savings stashed away. For my birthday and also as part of my wedding gift, Naomi gave me $150,000 and confided in me that I shouldn't share this secret with anyone. But now you are my husband and because there should be no secret between us, I want to share my life with you. I used part of this money for the wedding and I also want to use the rest for us. It's hard when you don't have a family to depend on, and as a bride, the wedding was my responsibility…Naomi, as a mother, was just looking out for me." With tear-filled eyes and a determined look of appreciation for Naomi, Ruth took Otis's hand and pleaded with him, "I hope you understand."

The cracks in her voice touched Otis's heart as he pictured the humility to which Ruth had surrendered, and how gracefully she had carried herself throughout the wedding preparation and ceremony. "That's alright, Babe, Naomi has a great heart." Otis continued, with a gentle smile across his lips to ease away Ruth's fears, "But you'd let me know if you needed help, right?"

"Oh, Honey, trust me…I will," Ruth remarked, with a smile. And with a kiss, she took on the responsibility of providing for her family for the next six months.

That evening, Ruth was so excited. She wanted to share the moment with Brian, Marcus and Naomi, so the couple drove back to Naomi's. But since it was getting a little late, Naomi gracefully declined and asked Ruth to take her over to the new home the following day. Brian and Marcus, however, were up for it, so Ruth and Otis drove back to their estate with the boys, who were as excited as their mom.

Still on vacation the next day, Otis joined Ruth, Naomi and the boys as they went through all the cards and gifts from the wedding. The next couple of weeks came with a lot of work for the entire family, as they had to move to their new home, decorate, send out thank you cards, and host a wedding party for close friends over at Otis's place. Ruth decided to rent out her old home to a former co-worker so that she could have a steady income stream to take care of needs she didn't want to be a bother for Otis. He, on the other hand, sold his property and invested the profit from the sale in the stock market, with the returns to go into Brian and Marcus's college fund. The transition was fun for the boys and somewhat hectic for Ruth and Otis, who had to return to work and check up on his patients.

Naomi was there by Ruth's side each step of the way as they went shopping for decorations for the new place. She offered suggestions of color schemes and décor. Naomi even bought some paintings she considered priceless and ageless for her daughter's new home. She always seized whatever opportunity she had to impart some words of wisdom into the life of her daughter, and during their shopping expeditions, she cautioned Ruth.

"Not everyone who smiles at you means well, my dear…so be careful of who you let into your home. As the woman of the house, it is your place to protect your home. Men sometimes overlook certain things that we as ladies notice. Always pray that the Lord will continually strengthen your spirit of discernment. You did not marry a man with a lot of family ties, but all the same, be careful of the so-called 'friends,' both male and female, who would seem to like you a little bit too much. I'm not sure you have a lot of girlfriends, but if for whatever reason in life you are tempted to have a female friend or two that you think you should trust, still be careful, Baby. Trust me on this one…I know what I am talking about. I had to learn some things the hard way, but for the grace of God."

There was a brief silence and then Naomi continued. "Guard your tongue. It can be an unruly evil…don't let your mouth abort your blessings…try not to react to things your senses present you, but respond…always put some thought into all your actions. This is a big step both you and Otis have taken, so make sure you two enjoy every moment of your life together. Tomorrow is not promised, so live without regrets. Always try to do things that each other likes and things that would make you laugh. Don't settle for monotony, be creative in your everyday life, not just on special occasions. Yes, it takes a lot of work, but that's the difference between staying married and getting a divorce. Don't let something or someone else pique your partner's interest. Do fun stuff; make sure laughter is always around. Quiet as it's kept, breathing and laughter are key components to a healthy lifestyle, and happiness, of course, is key to a lasting friendship, which I have found most marriages are missing these days.

"Now that you have the man, and you are confident of yourself, don't let anyone or anything drive you into jealousy. If Otis loves you as much as you and I know he does, don't worry about him putting anyone or anything ahead of the love you share. That won't happen. If it is God-ordained, make it God-maintained. You two need to be in one accord. Don't let the children come between you… kids always have a way manipulating situations just to get what they want, so always discuss each choice with your spouse before you two take any action involving the kids. Again, don't put off whatever opportunity you have to communicate with your spouse, don't say he or she will get over it…if he is silent or things are bothering him, resolve it before you go to bed that night. If, on the other hand, you have an issue with him, still resolve it before you go to bed that night. If your spouse loves you as much as he says he does, he would want to resolve whatever issue comes up. Always let you husband know that you love and respect him by the way you treat and speak to him; even during or after a disagreement and especially when in public.

"If only this world could know how important it is to communicate with that special someone in our lives…by communicating, you can get to know your partner and he or she will also get to know you. Therefore, you two can get to understand each other better.

"Baby, make sure you two look out for each other, regardless of what the world throws at you. Otis should cover your weaknesses, and you his. Again, don't let anyone come between you two…there should be no place for 'he said, she said' in your marriage. Ruth, honey, I know they say that marriage is a fifty-fifty partnership, but that's not true, my dear. Both you and Otis need to give 100% to each other, regardless of what the other person does. You have made a commitment not just to each other, but also to God. Do your part, and even if your partner is falling back, by your fruit and testimony, he will pick up the ball and give it all he's got. I will be honest with you, if he is slacking off and taking you for granted, there is a fundamental flaw in your union that the Holy Spirit would have revealed to you before you got married, and you chose to ignore…but I know that's not the case with you and Otis.

"As a wife and mother, always watch your attitude, my dear. The energy you emit and the attitude you exhibit will betray you, and folks around you will know when you've quit trying to improve yourself and your marriage. Never let yourself go. By that I mean your body, mind, and spirit. And never stop trying to maintain, if not improve, your livelihood and that of your family. Okay?

"These days, we hear a lot about marriages and couples breaking up because of 'irreconcilable differences.' What kind of nonsense is that? For one thing, pride can do that to you…oh yeah…pride, for sure. God hates a prideful heart, Ruth. There will always be things that both you and Otis don't agree about. That's okay…you are not machines…no two people are alike. When that happens, you can agree to disagree, but don't let it tear you apart. Short of adultery, which erases a level of trust that is hard to regain, nothing else is worth a separation or divorce. I say that because if we are honest with ourselves, we may forgive and sometimes forget, but the trust once had before the infidelity would have long taken flight. At the back of your mind will always be the knowledge that your partner was unfaithful and could be again, if put in the same position. Some may choose to live with it, and some may not be able to handle the disappointment that comes with it. I fault none. However, I know that won't be a problem for either of you; right?"

Ruth nodded.

"Whenever you are at an impasse that could have a significant impact on your relationship or marriage, you need to ask yourself, 'What am I willing to lose? What is the basis of my relationship?' Look at your state of nature, my dear. Examine your opportunity cost…what can you control, what factors are outside your control, and what would you trade for what you want? How strong is the foundation upon which your relationship is built? Sometimes we make the mistake of thinking that some things or issues are beyond our control, when in fact, they may be difficult to handle but can be accomplished. Always remember that by yourself, you can do nothing…but with God, all things are possible. Lean on God, Baby… there is nothing too hard for him. If your marriage or relationship is built on the Word of God, commit it to fervent prayer and let God have his way. If it's God-ordained, then make it God-maintained. Please don't make the mistake to which some Christians fall prey — we wait until it is 'mission critical' before remembering to invite

God into our issues. Always remember to be diligent in fasting and praying in every area of your life, as often as possible. By that, I mean prepare for war in peace time, Ruth.

"Honey, there are a lot of things we have discussed. We have had a lot of conversations and I am proud to see that you are a mature and self-respecting lady. You are a lovely wife and a wonderful mother, and I am glad to call you my daughter and friend. Don't let anyone take that from you. God knows your faithfulness and sees your heart. He's heard your cries and is giving you double for your troubles, so love your husband and your family with all your heart and always be mindful to give God all the praise in all things. I know these are things you are already aware of, but I think it's safe for me to go over them again. Keep Christ the center of your home...the family that prays together stays together. Schedule some Bible study time each week for the entire family. If your partner does not want to do that, then it's obvious you two are unevenly yoked...but this is not something we'd have to worry about now, is it, dear?"

To which Ruth replied, "No we don't!"

"Remember, honey, marriage is not an affair. When you two said, 'I do,' you were in essence sealing your promises to each other. In other words, you were putting, 'yea' and 'amen' to your vows, and you know what that means. You know, Ruth, of all the things I've said, let these passages of scripture — Matthew 7:12, and Galatians 5:22 and 23 — be evident in your life. Let them always stay with you. They should reflect the essence of your being, so read these verses, memorize them, practice them, use them and teach them to others, okay? Baby, that's all there is to living right. That's all."

Pondering those words, Ruth knew that her path with Naomi was God-ordained and she quietly thanked the Lord for his sovereign hand.

Ruth was the queen of the castle. She handled her responsibilities very well, and this bargain shopper got her money's worth while handling the finances in her family. Their home was elegantly decorated, bills were all paid on time, the yard was well kept, and the new house had become a warm home for Ruth and her family. However, before the fifth month was upon them, Ruth realized that she was down to $25,000 from the $150,000 she thought she had to spend and save for the boys' college. She was disappointed that she didn't get to save as much as she wanted from this money.

Otis had wanted the family to host a housewarming celebration with even the boys inviting their friends, but Ruth was not about to foot the bill on this party, not with her limited budget…no, sorry Sir…not on her watch! She graciously explained to Otis that she thought they should wait until their home was fully furnished, citing that it would be a bad reflection on her since the basement furniture was on back-order and the bar was not fully stocked.

Putting what was left of her pride aside, one night while in bed, Ruth snuggled next to Otis and with laughter in her eyes and in a whining playful voice, she began, "Honey remember when you said that if I needed help I should ask…well, I need you now…can you take over the bills for me a month earlier?"

"Baby…you have done more than enough. I really appreciate you furnishing the home, taking care of the house, cooking, cleaning, and you have been great…and it won't be any problem for me to step in…I am proud of you," replied Otis.

"Thanks, Baby…also, I know you have stated that you like what I've done with the place…don't spare my feelings, now…is there anything, color scheme, décor or furniture, that you are not crazy about?" Ruth asked.

"Are you kidding me? I think you have done an awesome job with this place…you make me long to come home every day, Baby…I love everything about it, Mrs. Swift."

"Thanks, Baby, that means a lot to me." Ruth responded, then kissed her husband…the prelude to a night of passion.

# Wisdom's Counsel

*"I count him braver who overcomes his desires than him who overcomes his enemies; for the hardest victory is victory over self."*
— *Aristotle*

The sight of Otis and Ruth was evidence enough that they were one with each other. Love was in the air. They completed each other's sentences, anticipated each other's needs, smiled at the thought of each other with laughter in their eyes. The seconds stayed, the minutes lingered, and the hours crawled just so that their time in love could stand still. Naomi was happy for the couple, but never really had much time to sit and talk with Otis, as most of their conversations were about her health and what the newlyweds had planned for their upcoming weekends.

One rainy day while making a house call to Naomi, Otis was greeted by a familiar tone as they exchanged pleasantries. It was the voice of caring concern that he had come to appreciate over the years. The voice that guided him during his difficult days, when love was but a lonely ray peering through the stormy clouds of his divorce.

"Otis!" Naomi started. "I am proud of you, Son...I always knew you would make it. Look at you! Oh, how I wish your father was alive to see what a fine and exceptional gentleman you have grown up to be. I thank God every day for knitting us in his fabric of blessings." After a pause, as if reflecting on the goodness of God, she gently grabbed Otis by the hand and slowly escorted him from the living room to the veranda, where both sat and with eyes fixed on the distant bushes, listened and admired the syncopated beats of the rain shower.

"So, how's my girl doing?" Naomi enquired.

"Ah, she's great as always," Otis replied.

"And you?"

"I'm doing well, thank you. I am happy," Otis said confidently, as he nodded in agreement to his account of his life married to Ruth. "So, how are you doing today? How's the therapy coming along?" he inquired of his patient.

"Son, every day I wake up is a blessing for me. God has indeed been good to me...I can't complain...morning by morning new mercies I see...I am doing well and I am thankful to God. Didn't think I would make it this far...I am grateful," Naomi testified with a gentle smile across her lips. Before Otis could concur, she continued, "I know I shouldn't even mention this to you. You've probably had many conversations and counseling from the wise male figures in your life. Anyway, I'd rather say it than regret not doing so. You've prayed and fasted for a loving wife, and unlike that Jezebel you first brought home, this one is a godly, virtuous, Christian lady. You don't have to worry about Ruth, she is as good as it gets. However, in fulfilling your role as a husband and father, let me share these pointers with you…these are things I've noticed over the years that tend to put a strain in relationships and families. By the way, this is a privileged conversation, so let it stay between us and the rain."

Otis respectfully nodded.

"I know you've heard the cliché that marriage takes work. Well, it wasn't only meant for the wife. As you would like Ruth to respect your space, respect hers. As a husband, don't get complacent after you've said, 'I do.' Just like you put your best foot forward when you didn't know her in a biblical sense, keep it forward till the Lord calls you home. Keep being proactive in matters concerning the family and your lover's heart. By that I mean, keep working on thrilling your wife, in and out of the bedroom, inspiring her thoughts by engaging her in decision-making processes. Encourage her creativity, even if the idea in question is at best questionable. And most of all, treat her as the queen you know she is.

"I know you are not guilty of this, but I'll say it anyway: don't be judgmental and condescending to your wife in private or public. True, you may have more knowledge of some subjects or issues, but that shouldn't give you the right to talk down to her or keep criticizing her for not knowing what you do and not being used to doing things the way that are acceptable to you. She needs a husband and a friend, not a mean old father figure, who instead of gently guiding her in love will get upset at the thought of offering assistance to the one he professes to love. She is not your slave, and being a man doesn't make her your subordinate. Have patience, show compassion. No one needs a constant reminder of their shortcomings...not you, not me, not anyone. This is all about you treating someone else the way you would want to be treated...let me correct that...the way God treats us. If God has been kind and loving to us despite our frailties, who are we to be mean and bitter to another human being? Mercy Lord."

*Okay!* Otis thought. Over the years, Otis had come to know and appreciate Naomi for speaking her mind, even when it was uncomfortable for the listening parties. Through it all, she had gained the respect of her family as the wise mother figure who would stop at nothing to call it as she saw it.

While Otis was catching his breath, Naomi's loving lesson continued: "Don't let third parties have a say or influence in your marriage. Keep friends, colleagues, and acquaintances in their place. And remember, Otis, every time you flirt with someone other than the one you married and are committed to, you are disrespecting not just that person, but also yourself and your relationship or family. Please try not to put yourself in any situation where your body is speaking louder than your mind, and don't do anything to your spouse you wouldn't want her to do to you. Because you are a man doesn't give you the right to be flirtatious. How would you feel if she was acting that way to other men? Think about it...I wouldn't have appreciated it if Elliot had disrespected me or our family in that manner. When once you've said, I Do, Always Do: respect, cherish, and nurture the love in your marriage.

"Your obvious roles as a provider, pillar of strength, father, husband, guide, guard, comforter, counselor, burden bearer, and all that good stuff, I know you have mastered. And I trust as a good, loving husband and father, you are more than able to perform your tasks in protecting, providing for, preserving, and prospering your family. What I want you to focus on are really the little things that I know eat us inside, as women, that aren't much spoken of. Let's start with the bedroom. Please, Otis, please try to stay fit and work out. Don't get lazy in the bedroom. Be creative and spontaneous when it comes to making love...don't settle for the same 'ol monotonous habits in bed. By that, I don't mean swinging from the chandelier, but keep it exciting, keep your wife longing for and coming back for more. Make sure your presence in the bedroom doesn't drive her out of the bedroom...make it her favorite place to be when you are around. There is an infamous quote that 'women have sex for love and men give love for sex,' so make sure you love your wife in the bedroom even without having sex. Sex is great, but sometimes just having your arms around her, and a warm body next to hers is all she would need to feel that she is loved. You don't always have to prove your manhood...just being there is sometimes worth a thousand words.

And I don't mean just lying there like a stiff. Try to fight the temptation of falling asleep when she's in need of your attention…and no matter how tired you get, try to be sensitive to her touch. You cannot be a selfish lover either, son. This goes for both men and women…I had to learn this the hard way, but I thank God for Elliot's patience. You cannot be calling out: Please me! Please me! And then when you're at your station, you forget about the train that got you there. Never leave your partner burning…after a while she'll start asking if it's worth her time and we don't want that now, do we?" Naomi asked, as she peered over her glasses at Otis, who readily shook his head in agreement while wondering, *what did I walk into?*

"Let's move to the electronics: don't let anything come between you, your wife, and spending quality time with your family. If your wife walks by after hearing the TV and asks you, 'What are you doing, Honey, watching TV?' or something similar, let it be an indicator to you that she wants your attention...don't starve her of it. There will always be another TV show, another web video, another rerun of the top ten plays…so don't let that moment with your wife pass you by. Always cherish and enjoy your times spent together, and let her know you are always looking forward to being next to her. Show some interest in her shows and be patient in teaching her about what excites you about your shows, be it from the History Channel or a sports network.

"Help her in the kitchen and also with chores around the house. I know, I know, there is a myth out there about men not belonging or helping out in the kitchen…it's a myth, baby, it's a myth. One of the most refreshing things is for a woman to see her man contributing to the kitchen and household chores. You do not have to be a world class chef or clean like you have an obsessive compulsive disorder, but your presence and effort can go a long way. Yeah, some men can't even boil an egg, but it would be refreshing for the women in their lives to see love through the men's effort to please them. You see, doing chores and even working side by side in the kitchen does bring a couple closer together…you will see love come pouring down when you do…I promise you. Psychologically, how do you think co-workers are sometimes known to be more in tune with each other than with their respective family members? There is something worth noting about people spending time with each other to accomplish a common goal. It tears down walls, opens lines of communication, enhances friendships and builds a team. A man and his wife should form the primary team in each other's lives, and not let the outside world be the substitute.

"The jokes you know that were downright corny and that Ruth found hilarious before you got married are still wonderful to her. She may be the only one in the world who would laugh at your jokes, so feel free to be yourself around her. Find a way to enjoy doing the things she likes. Go shopping with her and be playful around the dressing room without embarrassing yourself and her. Surprise her with the little things and blow her mind with loving acts of romance. Compliment her as often as you can. Notice the little things about what she wears, her hairstyle, earrings, nail polish, and give her loving comments. She is your best friend, as so she should be…keep the friendship alive in your marriage. Nourish and cherish your friendship and marriage. Stand with Ruth and support her in all her endeavors. Don't just hear what she is saying or talking about, listen to her and engage her in her conversations. Communicate, communicate, communicate…I can't say this enough. You are the head of this family, so always make your voice be heard in every circumstance. You men have been blessed with a divine anointing in your voices. Walk in your anointing, Otis…walk in it. Always talk to each other. Discuss things that are not only comfortable, but also uncomfortable. Don't be afraid to share your feelings. Talk and listen to each other, always. Let her know she has a listening ear and a friend in you, and feel free to share your heart with her. I know that it's hard for some men to share their heart with the one they love, especially when their secrets have been proven not to be safe with the women in their lives. But you don't have that problem, Otis… you can always trust Ruth. She has your best interest at heart.

"Don't shut down when you have a disagreement. I know it is the solace for some men in trying to keep their sanity and stay civil. All the same, it is not healthy to shut down and not let the one you love into your heart. Like a fenced city, when you lock people out from coming in, you will find yourself locked in from going out. Come together as a team in arriving at decisions affecting either party or the family as a whole. They may be unpleasant, but always discuss the difficult things and include your wife in decisions that life will throw at you and your family. Again, communicate. True, there is a time and place for everything, and sometimes the initial shock of hearing a matter without a thoughtful process can cause havoc in the home. So, as a man, be patient and understanding if your wife's first response is not what you would have preferred.

"Otis, I love you like a brother and a son, and I only pray and wish the best for both you and Ruth. As the man in her life, you are the leader, as it should be. But in leading, always learn to follow… yield, when you must. I know you are satisfied in your relationship with and marriage to Ruth, but don't be complacent. Always try to anticipate her needs, and as often as you can, show and tell her how much you appreciate her. I know Ruth knows she can always count on you, but there will be times when she will need that reassurance. Take away all doubts and put her mind at ease, and make sure she knows that she is the one and only lover in your life. Always show her respect and love…be it in public or when alone in the privacy of your home.

"There will be disagreements along the way…no two people are alike…you are not robots. Make sure love and respect is in all your discussions. No one should be yelling or raising their voices to make a point. And make sure you never go to bed angry or upset with each other. As a man, Otis, you have to be patient. Patience is a virtue and it is becoming of a man who is mature and settled in his Christian walk. We women somehow bring the best out in a man, and the worst when not guarded. It is up to the man to exercise patience in how he handles each trying situation that is presented in a relationship. You do not have to be a 'Yes Dear' man, but patience will help you achieve peace even when all hell is breaking loose. Listen, think, respond — don't react. And when things seem to be overwhelming, be patient and let God order your steps. There will be times when the faults that our human frailties present will surface. For example, forgetting to meet an expectation. Even after you've apologized, and she says that it's alright and that she is fine, make sure you do your best to still make things right...no matter how trivial it may seem. Okay? Don't forget, forgiveness has nothing to do with consequences. Through whatever life's circumstances, always let her know that you love and respect her, by the way you treat her.

"One more thing: keep God first in your life and in the life of this family and marriage. Pray together, set some time aside for Bible study each week, and don't get so busy or tired that you both decide to skip church. Make sure that on any given Sunday, when you are not away on vacation or business, if one person can't make it to church because of unavoidable circumstances, the other partner is in church. You never want to miss that weekly blessing. Make God the center of this marriage...and if it's God-ordained, then make it God-maintained. Never leave him out of any major decision you make in this family.

"I know I have said a lot that you already know...the bottom line is, Otis, love your wife, treat her with respect, be patient, kind, and honor her, and always put your family first. Well, after God of course."

With a gentle smile, while still wondering, *what did I walk into?* Otis said, thank you. The two continued to look into the distant bushes with the raindrops pouring down heavier, as if cheering with a resounding applause to Naomi's wisdom. He was appreciative of the wisdom of Naomi, and like the chorus of his favorite song, he replayed those words over and over again in his mind.

# Harvest!

*"The heart has its reasons which reason knows not of."*
*— Blaise Pascal*

I t was the 20th of June, a year to Ruth and Otis's first wedding anniversary when Ruth found out that her menstrual cycle was already three weeks late. Her first reaction stemmed from a flashback to her less desirable days, and it was panic. That evening, Ruth drove down to the neighborhood pharmacy and picked up a couple of HPTs. She had suspected that something was strange when her breasts became tender, and her nipples appeared darkened. Thinking it was a reaction to the wild nights she and her husband had had lately, Ruth had brushed aside the thought of her becoming pregnant. But this time, the test proved otherwise: she was pregnant. She wasn't sure how to tell Otis, but knew that he would be happy and supportive.

"What do you expect? With everything you two have been doing lately…it's a wonder it took this long," Ruth mumbled as she worked alone in the kitchen to prepare dinner for her family.

Later that evening, she and Otis were snuggled on the sofa in the family room, watching the evening news, with Brian and Marcus in their respective rooms, studying. Otis took the remote, turned the volume down, and turned to his wife.

"Baby, are you alright? I noticed that you were a little preoccupied this evening and I was wondering if something is bothering you or if you wanted to talk."

"Thanks, Honey. I really do appreciate you looking out for me… I've actually got something to tell you, but I wanted to wait until we were in bed later tonight," Ruth replied.

There was a deafening silence as Otis wondered about the source of such concern.

Ruth turned to her husband, and with a somewhat apologetic look on her face she whispered, "Baby, I think I'm pregnant… I have been feeling a little strange lately, so I stopped by the pharmacy and picked up a couple of home pregnancy tests. They were both positive. I have scheduled an appointment…"

Before she could say the next word, Otis leaned forward and gave his wife a kiss. "It's great news, Honey… its one of my best kinds of news… Baby, you know I am here for you and will support you in everything… and if that means we are being blessed with another child, I am happy. You can count on my love. I can only give the mother of my children all my love."

Ruth saw the joy in Otis's eyes, and for the first time since they started dating, felt worthy of his love. For everything he had done for her and her sons, Ruth made up her mind to repay him with a child of his own, knowing how much that would answer his silent prayer. That night, Otis and Ruth entered a new dimension of love, and it was full of passion, even spiritual. He gave her all he had, and she reciprocated.

Accompanied by Otis on her visit to the gynecologist the following day, it was official: Mrs. Ruth Swift was pregnant. Since the sex of a baby was usually determined around the sixteenth week of the gestational period and could be confirmed by the twenty-second or twenty-third week, Ruth and Otis decided to wait until then before sharing the good news with family and friends, including Brian, Marcus, and Naomi.

This plan, however, was of no use, as Naomi called it the next day, when she commented that Ruth was glowing and that something was different about her friend. There was no denying it. Ruth confirmed Naomi's suspicion and told her that she had just found out about it the previous day.

The morning sickness was almost unbearable, and it turned out that Ruth was not carrying a singleton, but multiples…she was carrying twins. Sex: male-female, fraternal.

During the following eight months of pregnancy, Ruth's cravings ranged from Snickers ice cream and soft pound cake to dill pickle, potato chips, triple-fudge brownies, and sundaes. She also loved the smell of gasoline. Ruth was given tons of love and cared for like a fragile queen by her loving husband and sons. She grew bigger each passing day and her emotions were for the most part controlled, even though they sometimes got the better part of her. Missing from the action on some days, Naomi decided to move in with the Swifts, and was a blessing as she pampered Ruth. She watched over her as her own, to the point that Larry and Edwin's wives became jealous of Ruth. Knowing that giving birth to twins would be extremely painful, Ruth discussed having a C-Section with Naomi and Otis. He was in full agreement, and by this time was bragging and letting the whole world know he and his wife were expecting twins.

On March 4th, Ruth gave birth to Sherman and Sherri Swift. It was a joyous occasion for all, including Brian and Marcus, who now had a much younger brother and sister to protect.

Caring for the babies was a little more challenging for Ruth and Otis, but with the help of Naomi, all went well. The one thing both parents were never able to get a handle on were the odd hours of the night that the twins decided to wake up and breastfeed or play. Especially Sherri, who was always the first to wake up whenever the room lighting was down or too dark for her convenience. Ruth, for the most part, stayed up with her newborns whenever their dad had to be at work the following morning. Otis helped out on week-ends. Staying up half the night meant that by daybreak, they were exhausted and ready to fall asleep. Ruth and Naomi tried to train the babies to adopt regular nap times and routines that would encourage them to sleep through the night. That proved to be no use, as Sherri seemed to maintain her uncompromising schedule.

From the outside of the church, the christening ceremony for the twins, with neighbors, relatives and friends in attendance, looked like a full-blown service. With the exception of a couple of "full stretch limousines," the latest line of luxury cars were in display out in the parking lot.

Naomi never moved back to her home, and Ruth officially quit her job at GMNH after her maternity leave expired. She still, however, cared for Naomi, who had now become part of her family. Naomi, in turn, willingly assisted Ruth through the early childhood years of the twins.

She passed away in her sleep one quiet winter night, after briefly complaining of a nascent headache, when Sherman and Sherri were about four years old. Naomi's loss was particularly hard on Ruth, who wrestled with a brief bout of depression, but was able to rebound with the support of her loving husband and children. In the reading of Naomi's last will and testament, it was announced that Naomi's residential property was bequeathed to Otis; Larry and Edwin were allotted the family's commercial properties and investments; and but for the heirlooms, all of Naomi's jewelries were past down to Ruth; which didn't make Tammy and Stacy too happy with Ruth.

*It has now been a little over twenty-seven years since Otis and Ruth started dating, and the two just celebrated their silver wedding anniversary.*

*Otis is aging gracefully and looks distinguished. What can be said about Ruth? She is still so attractive...a gorgeous lady, molded in beauty and seasoned in love. Brian and Marcus never made it to Otis's alma mater, but ended up graduating from a medical school at an Ivy League university. Brian is now a cardiac surgeon and Marcus a neurosurgeon...and they are both married with children. Sherman and Sherri are both attending their brothers' alma mater, hoping to also graduate as medical professionals. Sherri became Ruth's girlfriend and protégée, inheriting the wisdom passed down from Naomi.*

*Of all the things Ruth has kept dear to her heart over the years, her journal with words of wisdom from her late friend and mother, Naomi, has been precious. From time to time, both Otis and Ruth reminisce on the great times they spent with Naomi and even laugh themselves silly with impressions of their friend, while lonely, silent tears meander down Ruth's cheeks. Naomi's words continue to guide Ruth through her marriage and life as she matures in love, and submits to her husband as unto the Lord. Otis is still faithful to his wife. Indeed, he has abandoned all and loves Ruth as dearly as Christ loves the Church. Their love never waned and the passion is still alive in their marriage, as Ruth found the way to keep her Swift.*

*As her family has grown and the love she shares with Otis matures, Ruth over the years has used whatever opportunity she has to impart the wisdom gained from Naomi and life into her sons and daughter. Teaching them how to be gentlemen and a gracious lady. Be true to themselves. Treat each other the way they'd want to be treated. And most of all, about love. Ever so often, while watching the sun retreat from its long day's work on her deck, a tear or two wades down Ruth's cheeks as she reflects on what life has taught her: the friendship and love she shared with Naomi; how time, with the help of the Holy Spirit, can heal all wounds; and that no matter how elusive love seems, the heart should always be prepared to receive it.*

# DISCUSSION

1) If we should not keep secrets from your partner, do you think Naomi was justified in telling Ruth not to inform Otis about the gift she received?

2) Discuss Ruth's endearing character traits that:

   a) Helped her form and maintain the relationship with Naomi.

   b) Caused her to find favor in the sight of God and man regardless of her past.

3) Do you believe there is someone for everyone and that love is available to all? If yes, why do you think there are so many single or divorced individuals?

4) If it takes more than love to be in a relationship, name some of the other attributes that you consider important in a relationship.

5) In reading and discussing this novel, did you glean any wisdom from Naomi's advice to both Ruth and Otis?

# RUTH's WISDOM JOURNAL

| *Until today, I've never met anyone who erased my pride; and yet gave me wisdom, strength, and purpose.* | |
|---|---|
| **Naomi's Advice** | **Comments** |
| *Is there anything too hard for God…?* | *As a Christian, I ought to know better…really!* |
| *With love, you cannot enter a relationship thinking or hoping it will fail, because it will. Control your thoughts, my dear. "As a man thinketh in his heart, so is he"… through our thoughts we impregnate our future; and when we speak, we give birth. Don't be cynical about love… avoid the negative comments and attitudes. You see, Darling, what happens in your mind happens in time, so be careful.* | *Wow! She got me on this one… this sure will account for most of my failures.* |

| | |
|---|---|
| *You need to hold yourself accountable in every situation where you find yourself. Accountable for your actions, words, feelings and thoughts.* | *Hmm! Accountability… okay, but what about those irresponsible jackasses? Who's holding them accountable if they have no conscience in them? Alright, alright, alright…I should only concern myself with what is expected of me. This is hard to swallow after I have been giving of all I have.* |
| *A lot of people fail to draw their line in the sand early in their relationships (I mean both men and women). They try to impress their partners by not being realistic and setting standards they'll later find hard to maintain; and when it is required of them to consistently live up to their partner's expectations, they retreat to the shadows in frustration. Don't let the moment set the pace. Set your boundaries early…don't wait until after he's come to expect certain patterns, then you try to change up on him. That is a common mistake that goes unnoticed* | *I know that's right! I should have put my foot down when Donald was bringing all those porn movies over. That's why he wanted us to have a three-some with my best friend.* |
| | |

| | |
|---|---|
| *You see, our values control our behavior, and our behavior is the basis of what we believe. You need to value authenticity because a relationship that is based on deceit is one that will not survive, Darling.* | *At first I felt Naomi was insulting me on this one, asking me about my values…but on second thought, I can see the wisdom in what she was saying. Actually, she is right. I've always tried to "outplay the player."* |
| *You cannot love anything or anyone else more than you love God* | *Tell me about it. But in all honesty, it is hard, though, not to love the one you can see more than you love God. I am ashamed, after looking over my life and thinking that I was such a good Christian, only to realize that I have not been living right. I know I have put a lot of people and even things in front of God. Tonight, I am going to pray and ask God for forgiveness before I lie on this bed.* |
| *Baby, don't be superficial and go for the appearance… appearance can change with time…or even a freak accident* | *Who wouldn't? That was my first reaction, but Naomi's right. Oh God, please let my soul mate be easy on the eyes!* |

| | |
|---|---|
| *From your list of needs and wants, you have to prioritize the qualities that are absolutely important to you as a lady, and a mother. The catch is, if a man can meet those needs, he can work on some of those wants, if he is in love with you* | *This makes sense. So I should first seek a man who will meet my needs…and my wants are the gravy… okay!* |
| | |

*It's not in his kiss, my dear. If that were the case, every good kisser would be married. You have to ask yourself, does he anticipate my needs? Mind you, that does not mean that he buys everything for you. Because if that's the case, only the rich will have partners. Is he a giver...does he give of himself...would he rather go without so you can have? You see, a man is a provider and a giver. For example, if he really loves you, the moment you maybe jokingly say you'd like something, it quietly becomes a project to him until he satisfies that need or want. Does he speak highly of the women in his life, like his mother, and sisters? Is he proud of you every day, every time, and everywhere...or is it just around certain people at certain times in certain places?*

*In answer to a simple question, "How do I know if he really loves me?" Naomi has guided me through questions I would have never dreamed of asking before hooking up with someone.*

*Life is not a game of chance. Don't hope for love — go for love. Make choices, don't take chances with your life.*

*I guess I never believed and acted on love, but just hoped that one day it would be mine. I now realize that hoping is a verb.*

| | |
|---|---|
| *Don't think anything trivial of even his jokes…they can lead you to where he is. Don't fall for the smooth talker, and be careful of what you show him.* | *Wow! This is an epiphany. I should have seen it coming, with Magnus cursing like a sailor, and me wasting my money on those short and tight outfits. That's what got me in trouble the first time. Wow!* |
| *Whatever you do, never try to manipulate your partner with your love, okay? That is what will lead to conditional love, and that's not what God has called you to experience or give.* | *Hey, what's wrong with a girl using what her mama gave her? Just kidding…Lord, I need the kind of love you give in this relationship and possibly marriage. You know this is my plea.* |
| *Pay close attention to him. It's up to you to train him to seek you as an intellect, a spiritual being, a confidant, a friend, a helpmeet, and not an orgasm coolant or steam reliever. Dress conservatively while you are courting him. You will train his mind to start thinking of you as a person and not a sex object.* | *Girl, I was wrong! I never really did myself any favors on this one. I feel dirty just thinking about it. Have mercy on me, Lord!* |
| *If there is something that he is doing that you do not particularly care for, don't be afraid to let him know it immediately. Again, draw your line in the sand* | *Naomi's told me this before, but I know this is something I have failed to do more times than I can remember…not wanting to hurt people's feelings.* |

| | |
|---|---|
| *You have to be careful how you treat each other, my dear, because "I am sorry" is sometimes very hard to accept. Especially when it comes to matters of the heart. Forgiveness is a process, Ruth. It is a painful process that's usually overlooked when overshadowed by lust.* | *Don't say...tell me about it! I still have some scars to prove it.* |
| *The only thing I'll caution you about is that when you do try to change a behavior, be a lady about it, not a woman. Choose your words carefully. You do not have to yell to be heard. Yes, you can outtalk him and out-argue him... but please, please don't raise your voice at him. Especially when in public. He is not your child...don't disrespect him. You will end up winning the battle, but losing the war.* | *Oh, snap! I am guilty on this one too. I have mistreated too many people in public...not just men. Father, please forgive me on this one, too. Help me be conscious and careful not to ever do it again. I have lost way too many wars.* |
| *You see my dear, some people would say anything to get what they want in the moment...and then later they come to regret their decision, and start looking for a way out...* | *Hmmm! I've got to pay close attention to that Otis. He looks quiet, but I can tell he's got his ways. For now, I will take it slow and make sure I keep myself respectful.* |

| | |
|---|---|
| *You have to make sure there are no loopholes in your relationship. That is what the periods between courting and engaging before getting married is supposed to satisfy.* | *This is just like what happened to Donald. We had too many friends and they were his excuses, until he was busted.* |
| | |

*Please don't ever compare the man you are with to others in your past, be it for good or bad, no matter how innocent it feels or looks…especially to him. It could make him feel insecure, if a negative, or it could inflate his ego, if a positive. And this in turn, even though he won't say it, will make him see you as being privileged to be with him. That can affect the way he starts treating you. You see where I am going with this, Darling? A man is a trailblazer… let him create his own path. You learn from your past, but every new relationship should be treated as a new book, not a new chapter. A chapter is a division of an existing framework, the continuation of a thought, sequence, or phase. A new book is a different story, a new beginning. Do you get me, Hon?*

*Wow! Every day I see what I have done wrong in the past by just talking to Naomi. Thank you, Lord, for making our paths cross in this life. And please help me to get it right the next time you bless me. If Otis is the one, Lord, please show me how to walk, talk, and act, so that I don't abort my blessing.*

| | |
|---|---|
| *Contrary to popular belief, a man is a listener and a thinker. He processes his behavior and words based on the hand he is dealt. He is not a mind reader.* | *I know what Naomi is saying here, but how come they sometimes act like they don't listen? I know some of those knuckleheads don't listen, especially when a game is on. I guess I should have got their attention before speaking. Oh well! I'll just file this one under "experience."* |
| *Men are just as sensitive as we are. Society tries to teach them to mask their feelings, but they feel too, you know. They cry, too, they feel unappreciated, too. That does not mean you have to put up with something you don't like. As I've mentioned before, you just have to let them know in a cordial tone, and as a lady, what you want and what you don't want. Find the time, find the place, and find the way to say what you want to say, and he will listen and do as you desire. Men are usually creatures of habit...* | *Hmm! Why all the hard core stuff? Life would be so much easier if what we see is what we get. "It's all about the approach?" What approach when there is a game on TV? This will be hard but I'll try. No one wants to be treated like they are speaking to a stone wall... oh well.* |

| | |
|---|---|
| *Be careful how you introduce a man into your life. They'd all say they are ready, but most are not. The fickle ones will shy away, but a "mature man" will want to step up and take his place. You see, Baby, a man is a protector, but you should want to get to know who is protecting you and your family.* | *Oh, wow! But for the grace of God! Thank you, Jesus! Now I realize that I never used to really take the time to get to know the men I have brought into my sons' lives. Wow! Look at all the pain I have caused these boys. Hmm!* |
| *Does he love you? Do you know that he loves you? If yes, then trust him to do the right thing. If he is one of those… And besides, be careful how you try to change someone else…you could end up opening the door to unwanted evil. With every change comes a new attitude, positive or negative. That is why trust is the primary key in any relationship* | *"Trust"…so easy to say, and so hard to do. I trusted Hamed, took him shopping, and then lost him to Sharon. Oh, well!* |

| | |
|---|---|
| *Sex is an integral part of a relationship, but should not be the basis for your relationship, my dear. There's always someone else who can do it better than the next man can. That does not mean you should give up on the love you have and go chasing the mirage of sex. Disappointment in sex can be fixed, but disappointment in love is a totally different story.* | *Wow! That's deep. But I don't want to be the one teaching a man what to do with a woman. Okay, okay…Lord, help me with this one. Can the man in my life also come with a few skills? Have mercy on me, Lord. I'm not trying to tell you what to do, just have your way, Lord.* |
| *It takes time, so let time work it out. There are many more sunny days to come, many more family times to enjoy, so don't try to make up for lost time all at once.* | *Lost time…if only I could get it back. I really wish I could make up for lost time. I have lost way too much time doing the wrong things. Lord, I need you to redeem the time for me.* |
| *Don't let him stay too long. Remember, you are a lady, and a mother.* | *This was a close call, but I had to remember my sons. And besides, I'd hate for them to hear or see me…* |
| *Don't base your love on a man agreeing to go to church with you, my dear. Contrary to popular belief, the devil goes to church, too.* | *That's so true! I took Magnus to church and then went back to his place after service. That was so wrong… on so many levels.* |

| | |
|---|---|
| *Like you respect your personal time, so does he. We can't be too selfish, and think that everything is about you,* | *Yeah, but she didn't have to say it that way. Oh well...I guess wisdom comes at a price called humility.* |
| *Your expectations are your expectations, Hon. You have to put yourself in the other person's shoes and understand that until you communicate your expectation to someone else, your expectations are still your expectations. Some people concentrate on sex and the pleasure it brings, while paying little or no attention to the other 80% of their partner's character and tendencies.* | *Okay! First I need to improve my communication skills. I can't be shutting down anymore. Next, I need to focus on things that will help me understand the character and tendencies of the man in my life a little bit more.* |
| *Contrary to popular belief, the shortest way to a man's heart is not through his stomach. If that was the case, only good cooks would have lasting relationships.* | *She's right on that. So if my cooking is not the way to his heart, and I can't have sex with him until we are married, then I have to find a way to tap into his intellect and emotions.* |
| *One thing you have to remember is that no one's love is worth you dying for. You can't make him love you. God can...so hold on to God.* | *I get it...seek ye first the kingdom of God and his righteousness. Bottom line: put God first.* |

| | |
|---|---|
| *In handling misunderstandings, be objective. Think with your head and not your heart or emotions, Darling. Don't try to make him jealous in the process. It doesn't work well with some men. If you love your partner, don't let him be, in the hope that he would realize your worth and come running. An idle mind is the devil's workshop, you know. They could pick up something you are not prepared to handle when they return.* | *In short, I shouldn't try to make my partner jealous or avoid him and wait for him to come running back.* |
| *If you know you tend to have a contentious spirit — for examples, as soon as someone mentions "A" something starts rising up in you and you feel the need to put up a fight for "B," even though "B" was not in the question — always make sure you ask God to breathe his "Peace" into your life.* | *Lord, help me not to try to fight my battles. Take away any retaliatory, aggravating, and contentious spirit from me.* |

| | |
|---|---|
| *Hold on to love regardless of the gift. At the same time, don't let him buy his way into your heart. If that's the case, only the rich would be in love. Just don't put your price up on the billboard.* | *Even though I want the finer things in life just like the next girl, I should concentrate on love and not what my partner can or cannot afford to get me.* |
| *Be careful how you use the word "my," going forward. Even if you own the house and make more money than he does, other than personal effects such as your underwear, watch how you use that word. It has the power to show possession and also exclusion. So be careful, dear, it could silently have a negative effect on what you have labored to build.* | *"My"…never thought of it that way. When I am married, there is no "my" in our home.* |
| *Just keep him in close proximity. Reaffirm your love for him every chance you get by telling him how you love him. If he really loves you, he will wait for you* | *I know this will be tough for him, and I sometimes need him so desperately, too, but I want God to bless this relationship. I have gone through way too much to let this one fail because we can't keep his pants or my panties on.* |

| | |
|---|---|
| *Before you and Otis say "I do," ask yourself, "What will I do or how will I ensure that my marriage is not like the others that have ended up in divorce?" You have to be willing to die to your flesh in order to make it work. Are you willing to die to your flesh, Ruth, are you?* | *Good question! How do I plan to make this different? Hmm! What should I do to avoid separation or divorce? Hmm!* |
| *Total submission, Ruth, total submission. A man should totally submit to God and his wife, and a woman should totally submit to God and her husband for this thing to work.* | *Totally submitted...wow! I guess this means no holding back from God or Otis.* |
| *Marriage is not supposed to be a union between a man and a woman, it is a triple bottom-line, an iron triangle, a three-fold cord. It is supposed to be a union between God, a man, and his wife. But couples usually leave God out of the equation and constantly wonder why things are not working out right.* | *We'll have to keep God connected or we will be disconnected.* |

| | |
|---|---|
| *Whenever someone does something good for you, be it man or woman, out of the goodness of their heart, with no strings attached, the most you should say after thanking that person is, "Thank you, Jesus." Don't abort your blessing, my dear.* | *I really didn't mean to offend Naomi after she showed me so much kindness. I am sorry, Lord, and from this day forward I will try to speak and be grateful when blessed.* |
| *When it comes to a wedding, it should always make the bride feels much better about herself when she can contribute to the costs, and not just the groom, no matter how rich he is.* | *Lord, thank you for, Naomi. Thank you for supplying my needs. I really was scared of the wedding, as I had very little to contribute towards the ceremony.* |
| *If you don't like certain things or what he tries to get you to your station, if you know what I mean, let him know it. Don't frustrate yourself and make him feel like less of a man. Communicate…* | *Communicate to him…that I will do. I sure want to be satisfied, always! Ha!* |
| *The underlying fact is that you have to be consistently committed in all you do. Be committed to communicating with your spouse.* | *You got that right!* |

| | |
|---|---|
| *Yes, a man should be the provider of the home, but don't let him do all the spending, and don't make what's his, yours, and what's yours, yours, either. Also, don't try to be the financial warden. He needs a helpmeet, not a manager.* | *With everything I have gone through, I can't stand anyone wasting money, but I'll have to make sure I don't become overbearing.* |
| *You cannot marry or settle for potential, my dear. Potential is just that: potential. It should take more than that for you as a Christian woman to give your flower or fall into sin, Ruth.* | *Hmmm! Mercy, Lord. I knew I was wrong, but couldn't keep myself from falling for what could be, and not what is.* |
| *Don't try to keep up with the Joneses or be in trend with fashion while your home is suffering. You see, finances are one of the leading causes of separation and divorces in marriages, so be on your guard.* | *The Joneses can live their lives. I will not let money ruin my marriage or relationship.* |

| | |
|---|---|
| *A fair percentage of successful women are having a hard time keeping their marriages or maintaining relationships, all because they don't know how to treat people with respect when success is on their side. Promise me you will treat people the way you want to be treated.* | *Yeah, I know I tend to be bossy sometimes too, but I'd hate to mold my man into a pushover. And besides, I want to make Matthew 7:12 my life's creed.* |
| *Also, don't get yourself frustrated over petty stuff, like the way he turns the toilet tissue or him leaving the toilet seat up.* | *I shouldn't major on the minor stuff in life.* |
| *Otis's friends may treat and see him as a "brother," but don't get it twisted. They may not be looking at you as a "sister," no matter how innocent it looks.* | *Wow! This is going to be a hard one to control, seeing how nice I am, n'all. Ha! Seriously, Lord, help me to always be on guard around other men and please continue to strengthen my spirit of discernment.* |

| | |
|---|---|
| *Keep your family circle tightly close. Watch out for the so-called "friends," and mind not to put the things you discuss as a family out in the street. Always remember that your personal business is your personal business, not anyone else's.* | *I need to guard my home against "friends," and make sure what happens in our family stays in our family. My husband is not up for discussion, and our personal life is our personal life.* |
| *Keep Christ the center of your home. The family that prays together stays together. Schedule some Bible study time each week for the entire family. If your partner does not want to do that, then it's obvious you two are unevenly yoked.* | *I need to keep Christ first in my life at all times.* |
| *You two are about to take your vows in the sight of God and man, and one thing I would advise you to do is to make sure you both absolutely agree that divorce is not an option. You have to be willing to stand forever, or you will not be standing very long.* | *Divorce is not an option. I will remind Otis that when once he says, "I do," he better mean it, because even death will have a hard time coming between us.* |
| *Make 1 Corinthians 13 the essence of the love you share in your marriage.* | *This is a good passage of scripture. I need to memorize it.* |

| | |
|---|---|
| *Be creative and take turns to come up with stuff to do in having quality time. Never stop dating each other after you get married. It is very important. Keep not just love, but your friendship alive.* | *I pray we never run out of cool things to do. I will try to do my part in keeping our love and friendship alive.* |
| *Remember not to put yourself in any position where your body is speaking louder than your mind. Don't indulge in flirting with men, and in these days, women, too, and disrespect your husband, home, and yourself.* | *God, help me to be a virtuous woman and wife to my husband.* |
| *Always watch your attitude, my dear. The energy you emit and the attitude you exhibit will betray you, and folks around will know when you've quit trying to improve yourself and your marriage.* | *Okay, attitude check is big time. I know I tend to get moody sometimes, so Lord, help me with this one, too. Also, help me not to get complacent in this marriage.* |
| *Be careful about the programs or shows you watch and listen to. These can feed your spirit negatively or positively. Remember, you are what you eat.* | *Whoa! I must be careful here. I am what I feed my spirit.* |

| | |
|---|---|
| *When you come to the fork in the road where life hands you a choice, always remember to make your decisions based on the word of God.* | *My decisions should be based on the word of God. Therefore, I have to study to show myself approved.* |
| *Appreciate him for who he is, not what you'd like him to become. We sometimes try to change our partner into something and someone else after we've become complacent with the person we fell in love with.* | *I should never be complacent or unappreciative of my partner.* |
| *Trying to protect the men in our lives from standing in the gap, we end up making sissies of our sons and impotent men of our husbands. Let him fulfill his role.* | *I need to let the men in my life be men, including my sons. I shouldn't baby them or keep them from doing the things they are supposed to do.* |
| *Respect each other's privacy.* | *This is important. I wouldn't want my man to be going through my things, either.* |

| | |
|---|---|
| *A man who knows his purpose is also a fighter, a guide, a guard, and a pillar of strength. He has a calming presence about him. He will fight for you emotionally, physically, spiritually, and in whatever arena his love is challenged. You see, he loves his wife as he loves himself and will take things personally whenever he perceives that his love is being challenged. But, Baby, all these attributes can be erased with constant criticism and nagging.* | *After I've got the attention of my partner and said what I need to say, I must not be in the habit of nagging or criticizing him. If he fails to act on what I've said, Naomi better be around, because this boy would get himself hurt. Just kidding. Otis is thoughtful, and because he loves me, he seeks to please me and anticipates my needs.* |
| *Not everyone who smiles at you means you well, my dear, so be careful of who you let into your home.* | *I know that's right!* |
| *Be careful of the so-called "friends," both male and female, who would seem to like you a little bit too much.* | *My husband should be my best friend, and I will not allow third parties into this relationship or our marriage.* |
| *Guard your tongue. It can be an unruly evil. Don't let your mouth abort your blessings. Try not to react to things your senses present you, but respond. Always put some thought into all your actions.* | *Don't react. Just respond thoughtfully.* |

| | |
|---|---|
| *Make sure you two enjoy every moment of your life together. Tomorrow is not promised, so live without regrets.* | *Keep things fresh…we should enjoy our lives together.* |
| *But don't make the mistake to which some of us Christians fall prey. We wait until it is "mission critical" before remembering to invite God into our issues. Always remember to be diligent in fasting and praying in every area of your life. Prepare for war at peace time.* | *"Mission Critical" — tell me about it! I have to stay "Prayed Up" for this marriage to work. Otis can't leave this one to me. We have to be in it together. The devil is a liar! Even Marcus and Brian will be praying.* |
| *You two need to be on one accord. Don't let the children come between you. Kids always have a way of manipulating situations just to get what they want, so always discuss each choice with your spouse before you two take any action involving the kids.* | *I should always verify what the kids are saying before making a decision.* |
| *Don't put off whatever opportunity you have to communicate with your spouse. Don't say he or she will get over it. Resolve it before you go to bed that night.* | *Communication…a big plus. I should not let the sun go down upon our wrath. Got it!* |

| | |
|---|---|
| *Always try to do things that each other likes and things that would make you laugh. Quiet as it's kept, breathing and laughter are key components to a healthy lifestyle. And happiness, of course, is a key to a lasting friendship, which I have found most marriages are missing these days.* | *Make sure fun, and friendship is alive in the marriage. Gotta keep things fresh. In other words, we need to be creative.* |
| *Now that you have the man, and you are confident of yourself, don't let anyone or anything drive you into jealousy. If he loves you as much as you and I know he does, don't worry about him putting anyone or anything ahead of the love you share. If it is God-ordained, then make it God-maintained.* | *Nothing should come between us. Worrying can't fix anything. So I just have to commit the marriage and our family to God from jump street.* |
| *Baby, make sure you two look out for each other regardless of what the world throws at you. There should be no place for "he said, she said" in your marriage.* | *Isaiah 54:17… in the name of Jesus Christ.* |
| *For all I've been through in this life, I am glad that Love still rides a broken saddle.* ||

*"LET US HOLD FAST THE PROFESSION OF OUR FAITH WITHOUT WAVERING; (FOR HE IS FAITHFUL THAT PROMISED)"*

*HEBREWS 10:23*

CPSIA information can be obtained at www.ICGtesting.com
Printed in the USA
BVOW021009250112

281355BV00001B/117/P